OTHER BOOKS BY LJ ROSS

THE ALEXANDER GREGORY THRILLERS IN ORDER:

1. *Impostor*
2. *Hysteria*
3. *Bedlam*

THE DCI RYAN MYSTERIES IN ORDER:

1. *Holy Island*
2. *Sycamore Gap*
3. *Heavenfield*
4. *Angel*
5. *High Force*
6. *Cragside*
7. *Dark Skies*
8. *Seven Bridges*
9. *The Hermitage*
10. *Longstone*
11. *The Infirmary (prequel)*
12. *The Moor*
13. *Penshaw*
14. *Borderlands*
15. *Ryan's Christmas*
16. *The Shrine*

BEDLAM

AN ALEXANDER GREGORY THRILLER

BEDLAM

AN ALEXANDER GREGORY THRILLER

LJ ROSS

ISBN: 978-1-912310-53-1

First published in June 2020 by Dark Skies Publishing

Author photo by Gareth Iwan Jones

Cover layout by Stuart Bache

Typeset by Riverside Publishing Solutions Limited

Printed and bound by CPI Goup (UK) Limited

*"Where we draw the line between sanity
and madness is a matter of opinion."*

—Richard P. Bentall

Madness Explained

*"Being in a minority, even in a minority of one,
did not make you mad. There was truth and there
was untruth, and if you clung to the truth even
against the whole world, you were not mad."*

—George Orwell

1984

PROLOGUE

Newark, New Jersey

Late evening

The lights were off on the porch, just as he liked them.

A guy could get a serious headache standing on his own front porch, Paolo thought, as he drove through the security gates and up the long sweep of driveway to the home he'd built, some twenty years before. With an assault rifle and a gap in the wall, somebody could get a nice, clean shot before he'd even finished wiping his boots—and all because some bozo left the frickin' lights on.

He turned to his son, who was in the passenger seat.

"You remember what I said?"

"Sure, Pop. We don't talk business in front of Ma."

Paolo nodded.

"Mothers, wives…they're protected, y'understand? We don't sully them with it, and then there's nothin' to worry about. Sooner you understand that, the better."

His youngest son was barely eighteen but old enough to be a man, as far as Paolo was concerned. Paolo had lost it to his father's mistress at the tender age of thirteen and hadn't looked back since, but Luca...

Luca was dragging his heels, and the family were starting to notice.

"You make it with that little parakeet, yet?"

His son shifted uncomfortably as the car neared the forecourt of an enormous, white, Neoclassical house, with stucco columns painted in a contrasting shade of pale pink.

"It's not like that," he said, awkwardly. "Janey an' me, we're just friends."

Paolo frowned, trying to compute what he'd just been told. Sure, he spoke to Lorena about this and that—and told his girlfriends a lot more—but *friends*?

The thought made him laugh.

Then another thought crossed his mind, so horrifying it stopped his heart.

"Boy, you better not be a fag," he spat.

Luca closed his eyes briefly, then opened them again, staring directly ahead through the car's windshield.

"No," he said dully. "Course not, Pop. I'd never be...a..."

"Say it," Paolo growled. "*Say the words.*"

Luca felt a ripple of fear. He'd known it would be hard, the truth he'd only recently discovered about himself. He'd barely accepted it before his mind had begun to reject it—if only to prevent that look in his father's eye.

His father, the mafia boss, for whom homosexuality was anathema. Something abhorrent and unnatural, worthy of ridicule and, in some cases, much worse.

"I'm not a fag," he repeated, robotically.

"Damn right you're not," Paolo muttered, bringing the car to an abrupt halt. "I don't wanna hear about no more *friends*. You better find yourself a girl with the biggest pair o' tits from here to Harlem, or I'll find one for you."

With that, he slammed out of the car, leaving his son and the bodyguard, who had remained silent throughout the exchange, to trail after him.

Paolo's mood was not improved when he entered the house.

There was no welcome party, and no sign of any household staff.

"Where the hell is everybody?"

He threw his overcoat on the back of an ornately-carved chair and planted his feet.

"Lorena!" he bellowed.

Silence.

In thirty years of marriage, his wife had never failed to meet him at the door. He turned to his bodyguard—a heavy-set young man who also happened to be one of his sons, though he'd never acknowledge the fact.

"Andy? Check the house. Somethin' don't feel right."

There was a crash overhead.

"The bedroom," Andy said, and took the stairs two at a time, speaking swiftly into his radio. A moment later, three more men burst into the house and fanned out, checking every room.

Paolo sank onto a nearby chair and ran a tired hand over his face.

"Shouldn't we check on Ma?" Luca asked, casting his eyes towards the ceiling as they heard the sound of the men's thundering footsteps. "If she's in trouble—"

Andy's voice interrupted them from the landing upstairs.

"You better come quick, Mr Romano."

The first time Paolo Romano had seen a stiff had been on the afternoon of his fifth birthday, when he'd watched his father take a gun out of the pocket of his terry-towelling robe and shoot the pool boy, who he'd said had looked at him 'funny'.

Lazy bastard, his father had said, before toeing the body into the turquoise blue water, where it landed with a splash.

He'd never forget the sight of those big, bulging eyes disappearing beneath the waterline, and had never liked swimming since.

Now, as he heaved his considerable bulk up to the first floor and along the landing to the master bedroom, Paolo tried to remember where and when he'd first met Lorena.

Funny, the things that stuck in your mind, and the things that didn't.

"In here, sir."

Andy had been around the block plenty of times, and barely broke a sweat when he was stuffing some poor schmuck into the trunk of a car, but Paolo could see the sheen of perspiration on his forehead now.

Lorena must be in a worse state than he thought.

The bedroom was in disarray.

A lamp lay in pieces on the thick-pile carpet, having first connected with the wall, leaving a dent in the flowery silk wallpaper. Chairs had been overturned, mirrors were smashed, and clothing was strewn all over the floor, ripped and torn. The bed—an elaborate four-poster affair, with heavy silk curtains—looked as though a hurricane had hit it.

But there was no bloodied corpse anywhere in sight.

"She's on the terrace," Andy said, nervously.

The terrace led off the bedroom and spanned the full length of the house, overlooking the garden. Paolo never used it himself—the idea of sitting out in plain sight for any period of time sent a chill up his spine—but Lorena insisted on having coffee and croissants out there most mornings. He allowed the small act of defiance, reasoning that, if she wanted to get herself killed, it was her own damn business.

When Paolo took his first, cautious step through the French windows, he saw that it wasn't a bullet that had struck Lorena. A bullet would have been quick, and straightforward. He would have told every man present to convene a war council, instructing them to find the perpetrator and exact swift, merciless retribution for the murder of his beloved wife. After a respectable amount of time, he'd have married again and changed the goddamn wallpaper.

But he knew it wasn't a bullet. A bullet didn't leave the bedroom looking like that.

"Lorena?"

His wife cowered in the far corner of the terrace, hunkering down beside a potted plant. She was dressed in the silk pyjamas he'd bought her on a whim last Christmas—normally, they were ivory white, but now the cuffs and hemline were grubby, spattered with her own blood from a spidery web of nicks and cuts on her hands and feet.

"Lorena, what the hell you doin' out here? Get your ass back inside."

She didn't seem to hear him, and continued to stare into space with wide, frightened eyes.

"Can you see it?" she whispered.

Paolo frowned, and shook his head.

"What're you talkin' about? You're talkin' crazy again, Rena."

"There," she said, and pointed a shaking finger towards the empty space beside him. "*There*! It's coming for me…It's coming for me, Paolo!"

He was starting to lose patience—and was embarrassed, besides.

"Get out," he told the guards.

The men looked at her stricken face, then back at their boss.

"Didn't y'hear what I said?" he shouted. "Go on, get outta here!"

The men filed out, too careful to let him see their smirks.

Paolo took a few deep breaths and uncurled his fists, fighting for composure.

"What're you tryin' to do to me, Rena? You tryin' to punish me—is that it? You leave the house like a sty and wait for me to come home and find you like this? You got no respect for the things I buy for you, the house I built for you…"

She continued to stare over his shoulder.

"Look at me, when I'm talkin' to you, goddamn it!"

He crossed the terrace in a few strides and grasped his wife's thin shoulders, dragging her to her feet.

"Stop it, y'hear!" He shook her until he heard the teeth rattling inside her head.

"Pop, she's not well—"

"You shut your mouth," he growled at the boy, who stood shaking in the doorway. "Go back inside—"

Her bony, pink-tipped fingers gripped his arm.

"Paolo," she whispered. "It's behind you—*oh, God*, can't you see it?"

Though he knew there was nothing there, he turned around in reflex.

"What? See *what*?"

She turned to look up at him with big, frightened eyes and, for a fleeting moment, he remembered the girl she had once been.

"The *demon*," she whispered. "It's there. It—it came for me—"

Lorena dissolved into hysterical cries, fighting and clawing to escape the hands that held her, and the demon that hounded her.

He came to a decision.

"Call the doctor," he told his son. "Tell him to come quick."

When his son disappeared inside to make the call, Paolo looked down at his wife's shrivelled form, crouched on the floor at his feet. Lorena had been beautiful, once. Curvaceous and dark, with those big brown eyes he had a weakness for. Now, three children and thirty years later, she was a shadow; a pale, wasted version of the woman she'd once been.

Pity.

He dropped down beside her, and took her jaw in his hand, as he might have done a wayward puppy.

"You been takin' too many pills again, honey? Hmm? That it?"

She tried to shake her head, but his grip was too strong, and tears leaked down her cheeks.

"Listen to me, Rena," he said, softly. "I can't have this no more. You're gonna get yourself straightened out, you hear me?"

She began to mutter incoherently—a hissing sound that ran around his head, taunting and baiting him to slap her mouth shut.

Luca hurried back onto the terrace.

"Doc's on his way," he said.

Paolo looked up.

"I don't want nobody else knowin' about this," he said.

Luca nodded, swiping a nervous hand across his mouth. "What're you gonna do?"

Paolo smiled grimly.

He'd do what he always did, when there was a difficult situation.

Handle it.

"She needs a nice, long holiday, is all," he said. "Somewhere quiet."

He knew just the place.

CHAPTER 1

Quantico, Virginia

Two weeks later

The Federal Bureau of Investigation had chosen to site their Training Academy at the epicentre of the Marine Corps Base at Quantico, deep in the heart of rural Virginia. That the FBI's cerebral core should be protected by the might of the US Navy was an interesting feature of the United States' approach to law enforcement in general, and the significance was not lost on any of them. When he was appointed as the Bureau's first director, J. Edgar Hoover's vision had been to create a collective of agents more akin to Platonic guardians—an intelligentsia, whose education and experience set them apart from the 'common herd' and to whom others should rightly defer. There was some disagreement on whether that vision had been realised and whether it inspired the kind of respectful deference Hoover had hoped for, but in the years following his departure, a sincere effort had been made to build strong working relationships with other agencies. To that end, their Behavioural Analysis Unit ran ad hoc training sessions with other law enforcement agencies and regularly hosted a number of international conferences, to which they invited leading academics, clinicians and profilers from around the world to engage in a diverse, week-long schedule of seminars on all things related to offender-profiling.

Doctor Alexander Gregory had been invited to deliver a presentation at one of these outreach efforts, alongside his long-time friend and mentor, Professor Bill Douglas—himself a leading expert in criminal profiling and a fellow of Hawking College, Cambridge. The mystique surrounding the FBI's internal operations meant that an invitation to Quantico was always to be greeted with a tug of excitement and a quickly-drafted letter of acceptance, and so the two men found themselves embarking on the fifteen-hour pilgrimage from London to a little corner of the world they might otherwise never have known existed.

The air was humid when they touched down at the airport in Baltimore, and stayed that way throughout the two-hour journey across state lines to Virginia. Faulty air-conditioning in their rental car forced them to lower the windows but, as they wound through the dense forest encircling the base, the breeze no longer carried the oily stench of exhaust fumes from the Washington freeway but instead the rich, earthy scent of pine—marred only by the distant sound of gunfire.

"I don't remember it being this hot, the last time we were here," Gregory said.

That had been two—no, three—years ago, he thought with a degree of surprise. Time seemed to be accelerating, lately.

"I'm shocked they'd have us back at all," Douglas joked. "Must be thanks to your infamy, and my notoriety."

Gregory's hands were competent on the wheel, as they were with most things, and his expression was one of focused concentration as they neared the Training Academy. He'd lost weight since returning from Paris earlier in the year, where he'd consulted on a high-profile and extremely rare case of Dissociative Identity Disorder, more commonly known as Multiple Personality Disorder. It had taken a lot out of him, and the fact they'd been invited to speak at the conference owing to the widespread media coverage of that case was something of a double-edged sword. Much as he tried to keep personal feelings at bay, a psychologist was only human. Some cases stayed with you, niggling their way beneath any clinical defences he tried to build. It helped to focus the mind elsewhere; on new cases, different patients, different problems—or on the mundane, everyday tasks that made up the fabric of life. It certainly didn't help to revisit them, time and again, as he was now being asked to do.

Douglas sensed his friend's disquiet.

"I was thinking of the first time we came here, myself," he said, conversationally. "Seems a lifetime ago, doesn't it?"

Gregory smiled slightly, just the merest tug of skin at the corner of his mouth.

"That was before the Andersson case," he muttered.

Theodor Andersson had been a serial murderer of male sex workers, operating mainly around the Soho area of London. Three years earlier, and not long after their triumphant return from another FBI conference, Gregory and Douglas had been invited to work alongside the Metropolitan Police to consult on the case and provide a working profile, to help narrow their field of suspects. Unfortunately, owing to a catalogue of investigative errors and a misapplication of the profile they'd created, an innocent man was arrested and tried for Andersson's crimes. In the time it had taken the police to realise their mistake, Andersson had been free to kill again.

In the inevitable fall-out, their little profiling unit had been the perfect scapegoat.

"There's been a lot of water under the bridge since then," Douglas said. "Besides, anybody in policing or profiling circles knows what really happened."

That may be true, Gregory thought, but it didn't help him sleep any better at night.

"I don't know if it's wise, becoming embroiled in profiling all over again," he said. "Didn't we learn our lesson the first time around?"

Douglas could understand his friend's caution. The backlash following the arrest and prosecution of an innocent man had been relentless. They'd been hounded, day and night, and it had taken some time to recover from the impact. But there was still one abiding and irrefutable truth— the profile they'd created had not been wrong. Misapplied and subject to over-reliance, maybe, but never *wrong*.

Which was why they found themselves driving along the lonely forest road to Quantico, once again.

"Between us, we have a special and unique set of skills," Douglas said. "The product of years of study and evaluation. Should we let all that knowledge fester, on the off-chance we'll be criticised again, or should we put it to use?"

Gregory shook his head. "You don't need to convince me," he said. "If I didn't already agree with you, I wouldn't be here."

Douglas nodded, watching the shadows play across his friend's face.

"I know you're scared," he said quietly. "If you want the truth, I'm a little bit scared, myself. Profiling always comes with some degree of risk, because it isn't an exact science, however hard we try."

Gregory huffed out a laugh. "I'd leave that out of your keynote," he said, and slowed the car as the Visitor Control Centre came into view. "The party line is that profiling is all about evidence, not instinct—remember?"

The two men exchanged a smile, which was quickly extinguished as a pair of armed naval officers approached.

Entry into the Training Academy compound was heavily restricted and came with a warning not to mislay the visitors' badges they'd been issued, or risk being shot on sight. This warning was delivered in the same friendly, upbeat tone they might have heard at their favourite restaurant, which was somehow more unnerving than the presence of government-trained firearms experts with twitchy fingers.

"We're not in Kansas anymore," Douglas said, with theatrical menace. "Hard not to feel unsettled, with so many weapons kicking about."

"It's no Emerald City, that's for sure," Gregory replied, tipping his head up to survey the BAU building, which was a triumph of beige bricks and blocky design, redolent of a bygone era.

"I suppose they don't want anything too distracting," Douglas said, and felt a pang of homesickness for the towers and gables he'd left behind in Cambridge.

"No danger there," Gregory replied. "I forgot how utilitarian this place is."

It seemed to him a kind of netherworld—the stuff of nondescript waiting rooms and airport lounges. The might of the military combined with the intellectual muscle of the Bureau had been forever immortalised on film and in books as something to be reckoned with. When Gregory was faced with it, he experienced a strong urge to rebel; to reject its rigid lines and lead a different life altogether, free of psychological jargon and form-filling.

If only he knew what that might be.

Gregory thought briefly of a woman with pale blonde hair and the voice of an angel, and wondered where she might be now.

Angry with himself, he shoved the thought aside and focused on the more immediate needs of the present.

"Come on," he said to his friend. "The programme said there would be coffee."

"It's as good a reason as any to travel four thousand miles," Douglas quipped. "Lead on."

The Behavioural Analysis Unit, known formerly as the Behavioural Science Unit, formed part of the FBI's National Center for the Analysis of Violent Crime. The Unit was comprised of FBI agents with advanced degrees in psychology, criminology and sociology, whose mission it was to provide support to domestic and international law enforcement agencies, in addition to their usual caseload. The idea was to develop evidence-based research and then provide training to pass on their understanding of how criminals tick, thereby enabling their fellow officers to catch the very worst and most complex offenders.

When Gregory and Douglas entered the building, they were met by two men, both wearing dark grey suits. It was a leftover relic of Hoover's day that agents of the FBI should adopt a military, uniform style of dress, down to a regimental buzz cut and, in the case of female agents, the androgynous styling of a loose-fitting suit. As with the architecture, distractions of any kind were unwelcome.

"Doctor Gregory? Professor Douglas? I'm Special Agent Hawk, and this is my associate from the BAU, Agent Johnson. We're glad you could make it to the conference."

Both men were above average height but, unlike their trainee counterparts, apparently no longer needed to satisfy any fitness requirements.

"Thank you for the invitation."

"We're looking forward to hearing your presentation," Agent Johnson said. "If you'll come right this way, I know the Chief is looking forward to seeing you both again."

'The Chief' referred to Unit Chief Ellen Walker, whose task it was to lead the operations of BAU-5. Each division of the BAU had its own chief, but Walker was the most respected amongst them, having served the longest and, consequently, seen more than most.

They followed the two agents through a warren of plain white corridors and into one of the larger conference rooms, where delegates would soon be arriving for an early-bird discussion of autoerotic fatalities and mutilation, over a nice continental breakfast. Work commitments had prevented Douglas and Gregory from arriving the day before, so they'd been left with no choice but to take an overnight flight from London to Baltimore, landing in the early hours of the morning. Factoring in delays and the subsequent drive through commuter traffic, they considered it a miracle of sorts that they'd arrived in one piece, let alone ahead of schedule, shortly before nine.

"Bill!"

All four men turned at the sound of a woman's voice.

"Ellen," Douglas said warmly. "It's good to see you."

The Unit Chief leaned in for a subtle air kiss—only one cheek was deemed acceptable at Quantico, and only on special occasions—then stood back to survey her old friend.

"You look well," she decided. "Life at the university suits you."

"As do you," he said. "I was pleased to hear of your promotion—long overdue, I might add."

The most impressive thing about Ellen Walker had always been her mind, but she also happened to be a very attractive woman of around his own age, with a compassionate heart and a will forged of pure iron.

"And this must be the famous Doctor Gregory?" she said, extending her hand. "I don't think we've met before, although I believe you met my predecessor."

"Yes, that's right. It's a pleasure to be here, again, Chief Walker."

"Ellen," she said. "Well, now. How about a coffee, before we get started?"

Gregory smiled, and wondered if there was a god in heaven, after all.

CHAPTER 2

There was a bar on campus at Quantico called *The Boardroom*, which was something of an institution in its own right. Many an important discussion had been held there over the years, but any agent or trainee worth their salt knew that if you *really* wanted to relax, you needed to get off base.

So it was that, after a long day of seminars, Gregory and Douglas pleaded jet lag and excused themselves to go in search of more salubrious surroundings. Like a couple of teenagers, they stole off into the night and made directly for the town of Quantico, a couple of miles yonder, where the promise of jukebox music and a carb-laden dinner awaited them.

The town had been built on the banks of the Potomac River, marking the state border between Virginia to the west and Maryland to the east. *Hoover's* was a small, flat-roofed edifice, named after the town's most famous alumnus and built on the main strip, down by the marina. When Gregory pushed open its scarred wooden door, they were greeted by Dolly Parton and Kenny Rogers singing of islands in the stream, and the comforting sound of conversation and laughter. The floorspace had been divided into what appeared to be 'serious eating' and 'serious drinking' zones, with wooden tables and leather-topped booths set out on one side, and a long, polished bar on the other. Stools had been fixed at regular intervals along its length and were occupied by a motley collection of men and women, dressed in well-washed jeans and tee-shirts bearing faded slogans like *Class of '89* or *Born to be Wild*. A couple of televisions had been fixed to the wall at either end of the bar, eliciting a shout or an exclamation every now and then as newscasters reported the latest sports fixtures, and somewhere unseen they heard the *clack* of pool balls. Gregory and Douglas stood there for a moment sniffing the air, which smelled of frying onions and barbecued meat, and felt like kings.

"I've been dreaming of ribs all day," Douglas said.

He might have been a Cambridge don, but that didn't mean he had a fancy palate. It was on the tip of Gregory's tongue to ask how he could think of eating ribs after the content of their last seminar—which happened to have been a case study on serial killings involving arson—then he thought better of it.

"I'll stick to pizza," he said.

One of the hostesses made her way over to greet them.

"Sorry to keep you folks waiting," she said, scooping up some menus. "Would you like a booth, or do y'all want a view of the water?"

Gregory might have opted for the latter, but any decision was forestalled by the arrival of two more stragglers from the Academy.

"I see you've found our hangout," Agent Hawk said, stepping inside the restaurant.

He'd removed his blazer and tie, and was in the process of rolling up his shirtsleeves, while his partner remained pristine and watchful, as if ready to intercept any bar brawl or public disturbance which may befall the little restaurant.

"Agent Hawk, Agent Johnson," Douglas said, nodding to both men. "Sorry if we've interrupted your evening plans—"

"Not at all, Professor. In fact, if you'd both care to join us, we'd be glad to show you some Quantico hospitality."

Neither Douglas nor Gregory believed for a moment it was coincidence that had led the two men into *Hoover's*, but they were happy to keep up a pretence for the time being.

"Why not?" Gregory said, and turned back to the hostess, who waited with a fixed smile on her face. "Let's make it a booth."

They spent a few minutes ordering from sticky, laminated menus, and a few more going over the events of the day, before their conversation turned to the real reason they found themselves tucked inside a shadowy booth in the heart of downtown Quantico.

"This isn't your usual drinking hole," Gregory said, when it seemed the agents weren't going to be the first to begin.

"Why d'you say that?" Johnson asked.

"None of the waiting staff recognise you," Gregory replied. "You asked for a Brooklyn Lager, but they don't serve it here. Where's your usual spot? *Sam's*? *The Tun Tavern*?"

Both were well-known favourites amongst Bureau staff, whereas, somewhat ironically, *Hoover's* patrons tended to be marines and their families. It was the main reason why Gregory and Douglas had chosen it as their sanctuary after a long day of shop talk.

The two agents looked at each other, then laughed awkwardly.

"Not exactly subtle, are we?" Hawk said.

"There's something to be said for honesty," Douglas replied, with a crooked smile. "Why don't you try it?"

"Alright, cards on the table," Hawk said. "We followed you guys down here, because we need your help."

"We were kinda hoping you'd go for *Mel's Fish Shack*," Johnson put in. "They do some great shrimp."

"Give us a bit of notice next time, and maybe we will," Gregory said. "Why the cloak and dagger?"

There was a brief pause while the waiter arrived with their food, and discussion didn't resume until they'd taken the first few mouthfuls.

Priorities.

Eventually, Hawk wiped his mouth on a paper napkin and set his plate aside. He glanced around the room, noted the people sitting around them, and then studied the two men seated opposite. The Professor was the older of the two, somewhere around fifty, but with the gait of a much younger man. He dressed the part, with his rumpled jacket and tan briefcase, but he was no walking stereotype. Bill Douglas possessed the kind of gravitas that came from long experience—the kind you couldn't pay for, and couldn't replicate, either.

Gregory was a different beast altogether.

Younger, sure. Good-looking, but he didn't peacock it about, like some. Quiet, observant, and a rising star in the field—but not so well-known that people would make him on sight.

In other words, exactly what they were looking for.

CHAPTER 3

"What I'm about to tell you is highly classified."

Hawk spoke in an undertone, having made another discreet check of the vicinity.

"Should we be hearing it?" Douglas queried.

In reply, Johnson reached inside the breast pocket of his jacket and retrieved an envelope, from which he unfolded a single sheet of paper.

He slid it across the table.

"This is a non-disclosure agreement," he explained. "One of the active cases we're working on is very sensitive, with agents undercover in the field. We need your absolute assurance that anything we discuss will remain confidential."

Gregory didn't look at the document but at his friend, whose expression mirrored his own.

"Look, you came to us, not the other way around. Why should we commit ourselves, before we know what it's all about?"

"We're not at liberty to disclose anything further until the document is signed," Hawk explained, in a tone that brooked no argument.

"Well, you've certainly piqued my interest," Douglas confessed. "I don't see any harm in signing a non-disclosure. Do you, Alex?"

Gregory skim-read the short document and found it straightforward.

"We owe a duty of confidentiality to our patients every day," he said, and thought of life back at Southmoor, the high-security hospital on the outskirts of London, where he worked. "If you feel our advice would be of help to you, I suppose it's just an extension of that duty."

They scrawled their names on the paper, and Johnson thanked them before tucking it back inside his pocket.

"I assume you're aware of the Romano family?" Hawk began.

Both men stared back at him, blankly.

"I guess not, if you're Brits," he said, with a short laugh. "Why would you? Well, they're a BFD over here—"

"BFD?" Douglas queried.

"A Big Deal," Gregory muttered. "Are they organised crime?"

Both agents nodded.

"The Romano crime family runs New Jersey now," Hawk explained. "Used to be, the Five Families had factions over there, but the Romanos ran them out, one by one. They're the Sixth Family, now."

Truth be told, Gregory's knowledge of Italian-American Mafia operations didn't extend far beyond the *Godfather* trilogy.

"I'm aware of there being five Mafia 'families' who run the state of New York," he said. "You'll have to excuse my ignorance, but our line hasn't run much in the way of US organised crime."

"The Bonanno, Colombo, Gambino, Genovese and Lucchese families have their own territories," Johnson explained. "They've got their own structures, their own hierarchies...there have been bloody turf wars since the nineteen-twenties, but we had a golden period for a while back in the nineties, when gang-related fatalities were at an all-time low."

"There was a time when the Bureau had four, maybe five hundred agents working on bringing down these organisations," Hawk said. "Piece by piece, we broke them apart, managed to get people on the stand who'd never have thought of it before. Time was, these wiseguys had an unbreakable code—"

"Omertà," Gregory said.

The Mafia code of silence was common knowledge, even to him.

"Exactly." Hawk nodded. "Way back, you couldn't get a single one of them to talk. Once you're initiated, the Code says you keep your mouth shut—even if you're innocent. But, back in the eighties, we had the manpower and resources to persuade one or two of them to break that code. Once that started happening, the power of the Families began to fade."

"Do you think that's really the case?" Douglas said. "Maybe they went deeper underground."

Hawk's lips twisted, and he nodded again.

"We got complacent. Partly, we thought the Families would never be able to recover the ground they'd lost. But, then, 9/11 happened."

"Terrorism became the major focus at the Bureau," Johnson told them. "We had to redirect manpower to where it was most needed. Things were pretty quiet in organised crime at the time, so the number of agents on that unit went down as low as thirty or forty. That about right?" He turned to his partner.

"Right," Hawk agreed. "There were times I'd come into the office and there'd only be me and five other people, plus some out in the field."

"And, now?" Gregory asked.

Hawk rolled his shoulders and sighed heavily.

"While we were looking the other way, a war began. The worst since Castellammarese," he said. "That power struggle was what split the families into five, back in the thirties. Well, seventy years later, another one happened that we knew nothing about till it was too late.

"Who won the war?" Douglas asked.

"None of them," Johnson replied. "It birthed a new family—the Romanos. We're calling them the 'Sixth Family.'"

"How did it happen?" Gregory wondered aloud. "How do you start a new crime family?"

"They weren't brand new," Hawk said. "According to our sources, Vincenzo Romano was underboss for the Lucchese family, who had the biggest stake in New Jersey. He kept house there and ran operations on that side of the Hudson, keeping the peace between the different factions so every family had a piece of the pie."

"Sounds...idyllic," Douglas said. "Relatively speaking, of course."

Johnson grinned. "Maybe it would have been, except for the fact old man Vincenzo was a crazy son of a bitch. Unpredictable, erratic...I guess, one day, he woke up and decided he didn't want to be anybody's sidekick."

"He usurped the factions," Johnson said. "Murdered the leaders and took a direct run at the Families, especially the Lucchese."

"I'm surprised he survived," Gregory said.

"He didn't," Hawk replied, taking a long gulp of his beer. "Vincenzo was gunned down on his front porch. His son, Paolo, runs the family now."

"Did he seek revenge? For his father's death, I mean," Douglas asked, finding himself morbidly curious.

Hawk let out a short laugh.

"I doubt it. According to our sources, it was Paolo himself who took the shot."

There was a momentary silence around the booth, and they took the opportunity to order a second round of drinks.

Talk of murder was thirsty work.

"Paolo agreed to whack his own father and marry one of the daughters of the Lucchese boss, to keep the peace and make reparation," Hawk continued.

"How do you know all this?" Gregory asked. "This is high level information, surely?"

Both agents nodded.

"We have a contact on the inside," Johnson said, softly. "It's taken a long time to cultivate the relationship and build trust—enough for us to start building a case against Paolo."

"Paolo himself?" Douglas said, in astonishment. For the FBI to be thinking of mounting a case against a known crime lord, the stakes must be high.

Hawk nodded. "Now, you understand why this is so important," he said. "If we can pull this off, we've got the chance to topple one of the most violent families for a generation."

"So, what's the problem?" Gregory asked. "Did your witness get cold feet?"

Hawk and Johnson merely shook their heads, like two ragdoll puppets.

"We had everything in place for a pick-up," Hawk muttered. "Everything was arranged to get her into witness protection, but she didn't turn up. We made enquiries the next day, and nobody seemed to know where she was, or what had happened. She'd been missing for almost two weeks, so we thought she'd been intercepted and we'd have another *lupara bianca* to investigate."

A 'lupara bianca' was the name for a Mafia hit which left no trace, such as dissolving a body in acid. It was a particularly popular method of honour killing, designed to dissuade wayward wives or girlfriends from seeking a life free of Mob rule.

"If she isn't dead, what happened to her?" Gregory asked.

"We spoke to every informant, followed up every lead, and all we heard was that the boss's wife had gone batshit crazy—their words, not mine," Johnson said.

"Paolo's *wife*?" Douglas nearly choked on the last of his barbecued rib. "I thought you said she was the daughter of one of the other bosses, too?"

"She is," Hawk said. "Lorena Romano has Mafia in her blood, and knows all there is to know about the consequences of speaking out, which is why this was a once-in-a-lifetime opportunity. Now, I don't know..."

He trailed off, looking defeated.

"I thought wives couldn't testify against their husbands," Gregory said. "If that's the case, what did you hope to gain from Lorena's evidence?"

"There's spousal privilege," Johnson agreed. "It's why most of them never manage to get a divorce. But privilege only applies to stuff that happened between husband and wife. If the witness is willing to testify, and the content of the testimony concerns threats they've received, or things that happened with third parties present, the lawyers can argue it's admissible."

"Even if things didn't work out in court, the information she could give us is worth its weight in gold,"

Hawk said. "Thirty years of inside knowledge gives us a lot to work with."

"What made her agree to it?" Gregory asked.

In his job at Southmoor, he'd met and attempted to treat all manner of violent criminals over the years, and had met their wives and girlfriends, too—at least, those who'd been able to sustain a relationship. Invariably, he'd found that they fell into three categories: those who were too indoctrinated or too frightened to free themselves and thus kept up the pretence of a relationship; those who were committed to a criminal lifestyle; and, rarest of all, those who wanted to rid themselves of the men they'd fallen for, or had been coerced into marrying.

He wondered which one applied to Paolo's wife.

"We've had an investigation running into the Romano family for a while," Hawk said. "We kept getting the same reports about Lorena, saying that she hadn't been happy for years. We put some surveillance on their house in Newark, and started to understand why."

The footage hadn't made for comfortable viewing.

"I made contact with her myself," Hawk continued. "Took a good, long while, but I managed to persuade her to move into witness protection before standing up in court. By the end, Lorena was willing. She gave us dates, times, locations…hell, she could even remember the colour shirt her husband was wearing when he shot some guy down in Florida," Hawk said, and some of his disappointment leaked through. "We were on the cusp of something big, and we'd managed it so carefully. I don't understand what went wrong."

"You said there were rumours she had some kind of episode," Douglas prompted. "Did you check the hospitals?"

Hawk nodded, and ran a hand over his aching neck.

"We finally got confirmation on her location today," he said, with some relief. "She was admitted to a private hospital in the Catskills, a couple of hundred miles upstate of New York City."

Gregory and Douglas began to catalogue the psychiatric hospitals they knew of in that area. Relatively few remained operational, their services having been replaced by crisis support lines and assisted living, with acute psychiatric care units forming part of general hospitals in every town and city. However, if the Romano family hoped to hide Lorena away, there was one exclusive, eye-wateringly expensive psychiatric facility that sprang to mind. Perched halfway up a mountainside and surrounded by hundreds of acres of forest, its fairytale setting and old Gothic style evoked images of Victorian melodrama, of clockwork oranges and experimental procedures that were the stuff of horror stories. It was a place shrouded in mystery and notoriously private, just like its residents.

Buchanan Hospital.

Hawk confirmed their guesswork. "The Buchanan is like a vault," he said. "People go in, but nobody knows who's coming out, unless they're in a body bag."

"Another member of the Romano Family spent time at the Buchanan, a couple of years back," Johnson said. "He never resurfaced."

"The official line was suicide," Hawk said. "But the unofficial line is that Danny Barone was feeding information back to the Lucchese. Instead of killing him outright, they found another way to get rid of him, without rocking the boat."

Gregory and Douglas understood the FBI's predicament. With limited information at their disposal, they had no way of knowing for sure whether Lorena Romano was suffering from a genuine illness requiring hospitalisation, or whether the Family realised she was on the cusp of betraying them and found a way to dispose of her without giving the Lucchese any reason to retaliate. Then, there was the question of how complicit the Buchanan had been in any, or all, of it.

"How much do you know about Lorena's medical history?" Gregory asked. "Have you been able to find anything out from the hospital?"

Hawk shook his head.

"We daren't risk it," he said. "If we start making enquiries and the hospital ends up being dirty, it'll get back to Paolo and we'll have endangered Lorena."

"Do you really think the hospital would be involved in something like this?"

Douglas was an honourable man, who had taken a Hippocratic oath many years before to 'first do no harm'.

Despite all he'd seen and witnessed over the years, he found it difficult to imagine that a doctor, or anyone associated with a healing profession, would knowingly diverge from that basic principle. Consequently, his default was always to assume the best, until proven otherwise.

Laudable, though that was, Gregory took a more realistic view of the world. He had no difficulty imagining the scenario, not least because he'd spent time interviewing the notorious English serial killer, Doctor Harold Shipman, before his death.

Money could be a powerful motive, for some—and the Mob had plenty of it.

"To be honest, Professor, we're not sure," Johnson said. "The hospital attracts celebrities and high-net-worth individuals because it operates on a culture of secrecy, so people having a blip or whatever can take themselves off to the mountains and talk about why mommy was to blame without feeling persecuted."

Gregory smiled, but it didn't reach his eyes.

"Studies consistently demonstrate a correlation between early childhood experiences and offender-behaviour, in later life," he said, mildly. "Sometimes, mommy was to blame."

"No offence, Doc, but we get a lot of violent misfits looking for an excuse. It's always the same one, too," the man replied. "*Mommy didn't love me, so that's why I killed fifty-six women,* or some shit. It gets old, after a while."

Gregory could feel a headache beginning to pound in the base of his skull, a dull throb that kept time with the beating of his heart. In his mind's eye, he saw a child's night light revolving on the ceiling, where prancing, multi-coloured dinosaurs moved around and around to the strains of an electronic jingle, while his stomach convulsed in pain.

Johnson was right.

It did get old, after a while.

Alex excused himself, and began weaving his way through the restaurant tables in search of the men's room, and the respite of a few moments' solitude.

"You look lost."

He turned to find one of the bar staff smiling at him from a pair of big, heavily-made-up eyes.

"No, just looking for the restroom."

"Right over there," she said, pointing a manicured nail at a door near the entrance. "Can I get you something, for when you come back?"

Gregory's head might have been pounding, but he hadn't been struck blind. He could read the most complex of verbal and non-verbal human behavioural signals, and it wasn't much of a stretch to decipher the message she was sending him now.

"Whiskey, maybe? Or how about something a bit more adventurous? I make a mean mai tai."

She folded her arms across the bar, leaning in to give him a better view.

"Maybe another night," he said, politely. "Coffee would be great, though."

She glanced at the clock on the wall, carved in the shape of an anchor.

"You have caffeine now, you'll be awake all night," she said softly.

Gregory held her gaze, and smiled.

"Perhaps I will."

CHAPTER 4

By the time Gregory returned to the booth armed with Amy's number and a mug of indifferent coffee, talk had turned from the psychological impact of maternal neglect to the more straightforward question of what to do about the problem of Lorena Romano.

"What're your plans after the conference?" Hawk asked. "Are you heading straight back to the UK?"

"I have a couple of friends at Georgetown I plan to visit," Douglas said, referring to the university in nearby Washington DC. "I think Alex was hoping to take a drive along the East Coast."

"Really? Where?" Hawk asked, too casually.

"No fixed destination," Gregory murmured. "I was planning to see where the wind takes me, at least for the next couple of weeks, while I'm on leave."

Hawk looked at his partner, then back at Gregory, who waited for him to ask the question he'd been gearing up for the past two hours.

"You see our problem," Hawk said, spreading his hands. "If Buchanan Hospital is controlled by the Romanos—or any of the Families, for that matter—then none of the staff can be trusted, and there's every chance it's being used as a way to filter out undesirables, outside their usual methods. But we have no way of knowing unless someone looks at how things are, on the inside. To do that, we need someone who knows what to look for."

Gregory realised what they planned to ask of him, and almost laughed.

Not a written profile, or some words of wisdom for the agents in charge of the case—nothing so simple as that.

"We need to know about the hospital but, more importantly, we need to know about Lorena," Johnson said. "We need to know if she's still alive and, if she is, whether she's really ill."

"Why don't you contact the regulator, and ask them to do a spot check?" Douglas suggested. "Send in one of your own specialists, posing as a pen-pusher?"

"The Romano Family has links with the Psychiatric Board," he replied. "A lot of their officials serve on drug approval committees in Washington, which decide the fate of new drugs coming onto the market. We have reason to believe the Romano Family, as well as several of the other families, have links with some of the major pharmaceutical companies. That being the case, we can't risk contacting the regulator if there's any possibility of there being a link back to the Family."

"So, really, you need someone with clinical and forensic experience to go inside and find out what's going on," Douglas surmised, while his friend remained silent in the chair beside him. "Is there anybody in the Bureau who'd fit the bill?"

"Plenty with the skills and experience," Hawk replied. "But the Mafia has a long reach. There've been times when they've planted one of their own as a trainee at the Academy, and nobody's been any the wiser till years later. That's why the investigation has been limited to a few agents, carefully selected and vetted. That doesn't mean there isn't a file sitting on Paolo Romano's desk containing all our names and faces, so he'd know us on sight."

"The safest way would be to enlist someone from outside the Bureau," Johnson said. "It would be highly unlikely for anyone to recognise that person, or to make them as a plant. It would reduce the risk of harm to Lorena, because they'd be seen as just another patient. In fact, they'd be our ace in the hole."

"I take it you've got some lucky candidates in mind?" Douglas asked, popping a salted peanut into his mouth.

Two heads turned to look at Gregory, who had remained silent as he listened to their spiel, his face shadowed beneath the dim lighting of a nautical-themed lamp overhead.

"Actually, Doc, we were hoping you would volunteer for it."

There was a taut, humming silence as Gregory looked around the booth at the three pairs of eyes watching him.

"Not a chance," he said, firmly.

"You'd have the full support of the Bureau at all times," Johnson told him. "We'd provide you with training while you're with us over the next few days, and brief you on all the relevant procedures. You'd have a solid point of contact—"

"Who?" Douglas asked. He wasn't about to let his friend walk into the unknown without some firm assurances.

"I'd be your contact, since I've been leading on the case," Hawk said. "We'd work up a new identity and create a paper trail, so everything looked legit. You'd be just another short-term admission. You'd gather whatever information you could, find out about Lorena—befriend her, if possible—and report back to me."

"This is an exclusive place," Douglas said. "What kind of identity could be created that would satisfy their entry requirements? It would look odd, if you had an Average Joe walk in there, because they'd ask questions about funding, for starters."

Gregory watched Hawk's face closely, and realised something else about the two men seated across the table; something he should have understood from the outset. From the moment they'd walked into the restaurant, they'd had an agenda. One they'd planned and prepared beforehand, designed to elicit a positive outcome for their investigation, regardless of the means they employed to secure that end. They must have already known that his return flight to the UK wasn't for another couple of weeks.

Like any other law enforcement agency, they'd done their due diligence, and had probably dived into the personal history of the man they wanted to work with them.

It was always good to have some leverage, his father used to say.

And, in their due diligence, they'd uncovered his Achilles' Heel—and would use it against him unless he volunteered the information himself.

He needed more time.

Time to consider how to tell his friend about his past, and the reason why he'd changed his name to Alexander Gregory. Time to find the right words of apology for why he hadn't the strength to speak of it before.

Then, there was Cathy Jones.

The mother who'd killed two of her children, leaving him as the third survivor with scars that ran too deep to heal, no matter how he tried. And, God, how he'd tried. In every session with a patient, every time he sought to help another human being, he also tried to help himself.

Until, one day, she'd walked into his treatment room as a new patient, unable to recognise the boy inside the man's body, especially with his smart new name. He should have told the Hospital Board and excused himself, professional rules prohibiting any therapeutic relationship between a mother and son, particularly with such a fraught past.

But he hadn't told them.

He'd accepted her as his patient and treated her, every day. He'd set aside his own pain to try to understand why she'd committed so heinous a crime, searching all the while to find a scrap of humanity inside her brittle shell.

Mommy didn't love me.

He'd lived with his own deceit in an attempt to heal them both, waking each morning with the pathetic hope she'd look at him and recognise the pain she had caused. He longed for that breakthrough moment, when his mother would find the clarity to look at herself—really, look at herself—and understand the consequences of what she'd done, and even feel remorse.

But that day had never come.

Then, one morning, he'd returned from a case in Ireland to find Cathy Jones dead. The nurses on the High Dependency Unit at Southmoor had discovered his mother inside her hospital room, a strand of wire rosary beads wrapped around her neck like a garotte. They'd ruled it suicide, without ever finding out how she'd come by the beads.

And now, thousands of miles away, the two FBI agents had discovered his real name. It wouldn't take much more to discover that he'd risked his professional standing, and deserved to be struck off—no matter how understandable, or pitiable, the reason for his deception.

Gregory locked eyes with Hawk, then Johnson.

"I'll sleep on it," he said.

CHAPTER 5

As darkness fell, Gregory and Douglas made their way across town to *The Waterside Inn,* where they were staying for the week. Much like the rest of Quantico, it was a middle-of-the-road, no-frills affair that relied heavily on panoramic views of the waterfront to counteract any shortfall in furnishings or ambience.

"I'm fit to drop," Douglas said, and gave a jaw-cracking yawn to prove it as they crossed the forecourt towards the inn's lurid green sign. "It's been a day of surprises, hasn't it?"

And there were more to come, Gregory thought. But not until tomorrow.

"Get some sleep," he said. "We'll see what the new day brings."

They stepped inside the elevator, with its faux-marble trim and over-bright lighting, and Douglas turned again to his young friend.

"Are you sure you want to do this?" he asked. "It's a risky business."

"All of life is risk," Gregory muttered.

"There's no obligation," Douglas said, unwittingly rubbing salt into the wound. "You're not committed, yet."

But he was, Gregory thought. Not only because the FBI had turned over a stone and found the secrets he'd tried to conceal, but because he owed something to his profession. With every patient whose life he improved, he felt he'd gone some way to paying back the goodwill that had, even unwittingly, been extended to him. Every minute he continued to call himself 'Doctor' was lived on borrowed time, until the Hospital Board discovered the grubby truth and stripped him of all he'd worked for, all that was meaningful in his life.

Worst of all, it would be his own fault.

For every step he managed to take forward, the spectre of Cathy Jones resurfaced, dragging him back again, but he couldn't go on living in fear and shame.

He was a good man, at his heart, and hoped to become a better one.

The elevator doors swished open with a metallic *twang* and they made their way along a carpeted corridor, lined with mottled prints depicting military exploits of the past.

"I'll see you in the morning," Gregory said, as they came to Douglas's room.

"You'll remember what I said?" the other replied. "You've had a lot on your plate, lately. Goodness knows what you'll find on the other side of Buchanan Hospital, so you need to be sure you're up to facing it."

"I am," Gregory said.

Douglas pushed open the door and began to step inside. "Bill?"

He turned back, looking every one of his years beneath the garish strip lighting of the hotel corridor. "Hmm?"

"I—thank you. That's all I wanted to say. Thank you for your friendship, these past ten years."

Douglas frowned. "That sounded like a 'goodbye'. Is everything alright?"

"Not goodbye," Gregory said, stepping away. "Just goodnight."

He turned and walked away, his footsteps swift and silent. Douglas watched him disappear around a corner and wondered, not for the first time, what could be so bad that his friend could not bring himself to speak of it.

Time would tell.

It always did.

———

Despite his body's demand for sleep, Gregory's mind failed to listen.

After an abortive attempt, he gave up and moved across to the window to look out at the river, which rippled like blue-black ink beneath a crescent moon. It might have been the early hours of the morning back in England, but it was barely eleven o' clock in Quantico, and the lights of the little town twinkled in the darkness, beckoning his return. *Hoover's* would be amongst them, and he had a vague notion of going back to see if Amy's offer was still open.

He thought of the napkin still folded inside the pocket of his blazer, and then of all the reasons it would be a mistake to call the number written on it. Even as he crossed the room to retrieve the little scrap of paper, he continued to think of reasons to say, 'no'.

He pulled out the folded napkin, turning it over in his hands.

He was free and single, with no ties.

He was a grown man, and she a grown woman.

He was lonely. He could admit that, in the privacy of his own thoughts. Wasn't that reason enough to take up an invitation of company, if only for a night?

Unlike Madeleine, the woman he'd met in Paris and almost—*almost*—allowed himself to fall in love with, there would be no expectation here of 'happy-ever-afters'. No fear of disappointment or worry that he'd make her unhappy, eventually.

Or that she'd realise he wasn't worth loving, after all.

Alex caught sight of himself in the long mirror on the inside of the wardrobe door and considered his reflection. He saw a tall, dark-haired man with arresting green eyes which were, at that moment, swirling pools of emotion. Laughter lines fanned out on either side, evidence that he could still find humour in the world, if not in himself. The first flecks of grey were beginning to show at his temples, and he was struck forcibly by the resemblance he shared with his father—or, at least, what he remembered of him at around the same age.

There were dark circles beneath his eyes and a sickly pallor to his skin, a product of insomnia combined with lack of sunshine and fresh air. There was a time when he'd go jogging before work, his footsteps pounding the concrete pavement along the banks of the River Thames as the sun rose over London's iconic skyline. But now, he struggled to remember the last time he'd felt his muscles burn, or the wind rushing against his skin to remind him he was alive.

Gregory turned away, looking down at the only other pair of shoes he'd bothered to bring. They were soft leather boots, cut at the ankle.

No good for running, he thought, *but fine for walking.*

A short while later, he set off from the hotel and walked briskly down towards the river. The streets were quiet, now, and the windows dark, but he felt no fear.

He knew what real fear was like.

It wasn't bogeymen in masks waiting until after dark, nor the silence of a lonely road in a town far from home.

The bogeyman was more subtle than that.

It came disguised, wearing the face of one you loved. It tricked you with a smile or a tear, until you learned to mistrust both. It was the quiet voice that sounded so much like your own, that every so often reminded you of all you had dared to forget. It might have been night or day anywhere in the world, and it would have made no difference.

Fear would always be there, waiting.

Just, waiting.

Gregory walked on, embracing the feel of the warm wind rushing against his skin, reminding him that he was alive.

CHAPTER 6

"What sort of ungodly hour d'you call this?"

Douglas rubbed the sleep from his eyes and peered at his friend, who'd been awake since dawn reading about the Italian-American Mafia before deeming it an acceptable hour to call upon his friend.

"Six-thirty," Gregory replied, as he stepped inside.

Douglas was unperturbed, and simply let the door swing shut again before shuffling over to a tray which held an assortment of coffee, tea and powdered milk alongside what might have been the smallest kettle either of them had ever seen. He held it up for inspection, eyeballed the crusted limescale on the inside, then gave a philosophical shrug.

"Coffee?" he asked.

"Yes—no, thanks, Bill. Actually, there was something I wanted to talk to you about."

Douglas set the kettle down again and reached for his glasses so he might see more clearly. As he'd expected, his friend looked ragged.

"You can talk to me about anything, Alex, you know that."

Douglas settled himself on the edge of the bed and waited, hands linked loosely on his lap.

Gregory looked at the tableau and felt an inappropriate urge to laugh; Douglas was still wearing tartan pyjamas and his hair stuck out at interesting angles, lending him an air of eccentricity that, oddly, suited him.

"Why don't I come back when you've had a chance to get ready?" he said. "I'm sorry for barging in like that—"

"Alex."

Douglas's voice was one of quiet authority, a tone he usually reserved for patients in need of careful handling. It worked equally well in the case of friends who were finding it difficult to share an uncomfortable truth.

"Why don't you sit down and tell me what's troubling you."

Gregory nodded, and pulled up the only other chair in the room—a rickety-looking affair, whose seat pad had been mended with a liberal application of duct tape.

"I—first of all, I want to tell you I'm sorry. This—what I'm about to tell you concerns the most difficult..." He paused, struggling to find the words. "It's the most difficult part of my life and, frankly, it's something I'd rather forget."

Douglas waited, endlessly patient.

"It concerns my family," Gregory said quietly, resting his forearms on his knees and fixing his gaze on the floor.

"Go on," his friend said.

Gregory sucked in a tremulous breath and looked up again. If he was going to say it, he'd say it face to face.

"I was christened Michael Alexander Jones," he said simply. "One of three children born to Catherine and Stephen. I had a younger brother and sister—Christopher and Emily."

Douglas said nothing, just let him talk.

"My father was—*is*—a very successful man," he continued. "He made a lot of money in stockbroking and, for a while, we lived together as a family, in Richmond."

He thought of that upmarket London suburb, and wondered why people ever believed wealth had anything remotely to do with happiness.

"My father was very authoritarian, with firm ideas of what it meant to be a man," Gregory said. "He also had very little in the way of personal morals. He left my mother, and us, soon after Emily was born. They divorced, he remarried, and we never saw him again. He lives in a mansion on Lake Geneva, now."

That trauma alone would have been enough to generate feelings of abandonment, but Douglas sensed the worst was yet to come.

"My mother was…she was deeply unstable," he said, in a rush of words. "She probably had been, all her life, but, when my father left it acted as a catalyst."

Gregory fell silent for long seconds and Douglas had begun to wonder whether he would continue, but then he spoke again—his voice so low, it was almost inaudible.

"She—my mother—killed Christopher and Emily, slowly and systematically, over a period of several months. She almost killed me, too."

Douglas swallowed the grief that rose up alongside a powerful urge to take the man in his arms and rock him like a child, and fell back on training instead.

"When did this happen?" he asked, hoarsely.

"In the late eighties. I was six, when the authorities intervened."

There were so many questions, Douglas hardly knew where to begin.

"Was she imprisoned?" he asked.

Gregory realised the time had come to bare all.

"I suppose, in a manner of speaking, she was. Catherine—or Cathy, as she preferred to be called—was diagnosed with acute Factitious Disorder Imposed on Another," he said, referring to what used to be known as 'Munchausen's syndrome by proxy'. "She was convicted of manslaughter, having successfully pleaded diminished responsibility, and spent the rest of her life in high-security hospitals protesting her innocence."

Gregory paused to look across, and the compassion he saw in his friend's eyes was almost his undoing.

"Cathy Jones," Douglas repeated, rolling the name around his tongue. "It rings a bell. I must have seen the case when it was reported back in the eighties, or read about it somewhere…"

"I may have mentioned her, in passing," Gregory said. "She was my patient, before she died earlier this year."

Douglas frowned. "I don't understand."

Gregory swallowed. "No, you wouldn't," he said sadly. His friend was an upstanding figure, who would never dream of overstepping the boundaries of his profession. It would never occur to him, under any circumstances. With a heavy heart, Gregory braced himself to lose the man he'd come to think of almost as a father.

That, too, would be his punishment.

"I changed my name legally, as soon as I could," he said. "All of my qualifications were completed as Alexander Gregory. The last time I'd seen Cathy was in the hospital in 1987, the day I was taken out of her care."

He'd never forget that day, nor the terrible relief it had been to know she could never hurt him again. There had been pain, too—the kind that came with knowing he was entirely alone in the world. His father hadn't come for him at the hospital, nor any day since. Solitude had become a matter of survival—he'd built an unbreakable wall that no well-meaning foster family had been able to penetrate. He'd succeeded so well in protecting himself that, now, he feared it was all he knew, and all he would ever know.

"I kept up to date with her movements, but I didn't know she was going to be transferred to Southmoor," he said, quietly. "It came as a shock when she turned up at my door, as a new patient."

"Did she know you?" Douglas asked, focusing on the most important part of the story. There were complex issues to untangle in the web Alex had created for himself, but he was beginning to understand what lay at the heart of it all.

A need to be loved.

"No, she didn't recognise me at all," Gregory replied, and stood up suddenly to pace around. "I know what I should have done, Bill. I should have made the hospital aware immediately. But—I—I—"

"You wanted to understand," Douglas whispered. "You wanted her to tell you she was sorry, and that she loved you."

Gregory nodded mutely, and turned his head away.

"I never told her who I was," he said, once he could trust his own voice. "I tried to treat her like any other patient, and applied the same methods, kept rigorous records. I hoped...I suppose, I hoped she'd give me some reason to forgive her."

"And, did she? Did she ever make progress?"

Gregory let out a harsh laugh, and turned back to his friend with blazing green eyes.

"Never," he said, shortly. "Never once did she accept culpability for her actions. To the end, she was a coward."

"And—what was the end?" Douglas asked, carefully.

"While I was away in Ireland, last September, she hanged herself. I found out, when I came back."

They were quiet for a moment, listening to the call of birds of prey who circled high above the Potomac, each man lost in his own thoughts.

"That's why you haven't been yourself," Douglas said, as everything fell into place. "You've been carrying this burden on your shoulders for too long."

"It's a burden I created for myself," Gregory said, not giving himself any quarter.

But Douglas hadn't been talking about the professional breach in choosing to treat his own mother. He'd been talking about the untold trauma of a young boy named Michael, and the effect it continued to have on the man, Alexander.

"You must be very disappointed," Gregory said, unable to meet his eyes. "I want you to know, Bill, that you taught me all the right principles. I couldn't have asked for a better mentor, and it was my own decision to step outside professional boundaries."

"I—" Douglas started to say, but Gregory rolled on.

"I've wanted to tell you this for a while, but I couldn't seem to find the words. I was ashamed of myself," he admitted. "But I'm going to put it right. When we get back home, I'll write to the Hospital Board, explain everything, and abide by their decision—whatever that may be."

"You may be struck off," Douglas said softly. "You're an outstanding psychologist, Alex. You help so many people."

Gregory nodded.

"The rules are there for a reason," he said. "No matter what my intention for breaking them, they were broken, nonetheless. There has to be a consequence for that."

Douglas looked at the stiff line of his friend's back, the rigid manner in which he held his emotions in check, and could have wept.

Instead, he rose to his feet.

"Yes, you broke a rule," he said. "But life isn't all black and white, Alex. There are shades of grey in between—and mitigating circumstances, in this case. It's the right and honourable thing to do, to contact the Hospital Board, and my hope is that they'll take those circumstances into account when they refer the matter to the British Psychological Society—especially, when they read the character reference I'll be providing on your behalf."

He let that sink in, and when Gregory looked at him, it was as though he were looking into the eyes of that abandoned boy, who'd lost so much. The vulnerability he'd always sensed beneath the clinical exterior he wore like armour each day was now visible, laid bare for all to see.

"You'd do that?"

Douglas crossed the room and put a hand on his friend's shoulder.

"Gladly. Alex, let me tell you a little something I've learned about life, and about people. It takes courage to continue in the face of adversity, and courage to accept our own fallibility. Sometimes, we might fall down. But you can get up again—and, if you look for it, you'll always find a hand held out, waiting to help you."

Gregory said nothing for a long moment, then stepped into his friend's arms to exchange a hard hug.

"Thank you, Bill," he muttered.

"First hour's free," Douglas replied. "After that, you can buy me breakfast."

CHAPTER 7

A short while later, Gregory and Douglas made their way downstairs, where they found Agents Hawk and Johnson waiting for them in the Breakfast Room. It was a large, functional space with a smattering of round tables and chairs, and a stainless-steel buffet set against one wall. Grainy classical music played from invisible speakers, and did little to mask the clattering of pots and pans or the pervasive smell of cooking oil emanating from the adjoining kitchen.

"Strike while the iron's hot, so they say," Douglas murmured. "It looks like they're not going to give you any more time to think about it."

With the stakes being so high, it was fair to say that Hawk and Johnson would have used all reasonable means necessary to enlist Gregory's help but, as it turned out, they didn't have to. Having already decided on the course of his ship, Gregory felt a deep-rooted obligation to help the FBI—particularly since it may be the last time that he was recruited to help *anybody* once he'd sent his letter to the Hospital Board at Southmoor. He and Douglas both agreed it would be a fitting end to a glittering career in' the field, should he be required to seek alternative employment in future.

Until then, he might as well make himself useful.

"Good morning, gentlemen," Johnson said, and both agents rose to their feet as they approached. "We thought it would be best to continue our discussion off-campus."

"Very wise," Douglas said. "Have you eaten?"

"No, sir. We'll wait till we get back to the Academy."

Ah, yes, Gregory thought. Their daily round of croissants and coffee, over talk of blood-spatter patterns.

"Well, I'm famished," Douglas declared, and went off in search of bacon and eggs while the others settled for coffee.

"Well, Doctor?" Hawk asked, after the social niceties had been observed. "Have you had a chance to sleep on it?"

There hadn't, technically, been much in the way of sleep, but Gregory wasn't about to split hairs.

"I'll do it," he said, quietly.

The two men didn't so much as blink, and their complacency would have been irritating, if it had been at all unexpected.

"Thank you," Hawk said. "We're very grateful to have you on board."

"What are the arrangements?"

Douglas returned at that moment, his plate laden with bright yellow scrambled eggs—mixed with cheese, it later transpired— on top of crispy bacon and a stack of waffles drenched in maple syrup.

"When in Rome," he said, cheerfully. "What did I miss?"

"We were about to discuss the arrangements. Do you have an idea in mind, for a false identity whilst I'm staying at the Buchanan?"

Hawk lifted a shoulder. "It'd need to be a character with good financial backing—preferably privately-funded, to keep things simple. A Brit staying in New York, or something similar."

Gregory nodded.

"Perhaps we could use my old name," he said.

Their lack of reaction told him he'd been right to assume they'd done their homework.

"It would streamline things for us," Hawk said. "Perhaps Michael Alexander Jones has been renting an apartment in Greenwich Village, New York, for the past few months. He's a British Citizen of no profession; the estranged son of a wealthy family, who would be privately funding his stay at the hospital, following a breakdown. That work for you?"

It was close enough, Gregory thought, but not so close that he'd be liable to forget he was playing a part. For one thing, whilst he had a wealthy father, Stephen Jones would neither know nor care if his son had ever suffered a breakdown.

"It avoids the need to create an entirely new identity," he agreed.

"We'd take care of the paper trail," Johnson said. "If anybody was to check, they'd find everything in order with Immigration Services, your landlord, even the little old lady living next door."

"And he'd be out in under two weeks?" Douglas said, with a thread of steel. "That's understood?"

"Absolutely," Hawk said. "Much less than that, depending on how quickly Doctor Gregory can strike up a conversation. We'll work out all the details for the exit strategy over the next couple of days, but it won't be a problem because you'll be a voluntary admission—not involuntarily committed."

"In the meantime, we'd like to run some orientation sessions, give you a crash course on what you need to know about Lorena, ahead of time."

Gregory nodded.

"I'll be posing as your cousin," Hawk continued. "I'll drop you off at the hospital and take care of the admission forms and any other paperwork."

"I could help with that," Douglas offered.

"With all due respect, sir, your face is too recognisable in these sorts of circles," Johnson said. "There's a very limited number of agents working on this, for obvious reasons, and we want to keep the circle small."

"What about phone calls?" Gregory asked.

"We'll give you a cell phone number to call, where you can reach me at any time," Hawk said. "There'll be a backup number, too, just in case."

"What about Bill?" he asked. "Can I call Professor Douglas?"

Hawk looked across at Johnson, who shrugged.

"Plays into the story that he'd have friends on the outside," he said. "It'd look off, otherwise."

Hawk nodded his agreement.

"We'll set you up with a cell phone, Professor Douglas. You can call from that, or vice versa. Never, on any pretext, discuss the investigation or give your last name."

"Just one other question, for now," Gregory said.

"Shoot."

"What if I can't find Lorena?"

Hawk looked him squarely in the eye.

"Doc, if you can't find Lorena Romano, then we need to get you the hell out of there."

On which ominous note, they asked for the check.

CHAPTER 8

Thursday rolled around quickly.

The remainder of the conference had passed in a whirlwind of activity, with days spent in the Academy Lecture Theatre and nights spent in briefings with Hawk and Johnson. They hadn't been joking when they'd said the investigation was 'highly classified'; there had been no discussion of the case in the presence of any of their fellow agents, which left Gregory not only with a solid understanding of Mafia operations but a healthy dose of paranoia.

"All set?" Douglas asked Gregory.

Since bidding farewell to their friends at the Academy, the two men had reconvened in the car park of *The Waterside Inn*, where Agent Hawk would soon be arriving to collect Gregory ahead of their journey north.

"I think so," Gregory replied, tapping the edge of his suitcase.

It was another warm day, and the sun was already high in a cloudless blue sky, its rays bouncing off the crystallised tarmac at their feet. They heard the distant echo of a marine display down by the water, and the rumble of a car's engine approaching.

"That'll be Hawk," Douglas said, and reached into his pocket for a slip of paper, which he handed to his friend.

"What's this?"

"It's another number you can call me on," Douglas said, keeping a cheerful smile on his face as Hawk parked his car in one of the empty bays. "Put it somewhere safe—quickly, now."

Gregory tucked it away, and raised a hand to acknowledge Hawk, who made his way across to greet them.

"I thought you already had a number," he said quickly.

"I do, but Hawk said it himself—you never know who you can trust."

"I—"

"Morning," Hawk said, slipping on a pair of sunglasses. "Ready for a road trip, Michael?"

Gregory looked at him in confusion, before remembering he was supposed to practice his new name so that it felt more normal and reduced the chance of him making a slip-up once he was inside the hospital.

Except, in this case, the name wasn't new, and his fear was not that he'd forget himself and use the wrong name; it was that his old name would slip on like an old glove, and he'd forget that he was ever Alexander Gregory.

"Let's go, before I change my mind," he said.

Hawk shook Douglas's hand and then picked up Gregory's suitcase.

"I'll put this in the trunk—I hope you won't mind me checking the contents? I need to make sure there aren't any identifying items, and swap in some fresh clothes to fit the part."

Gregory gestured for him to continue.

"Be my guest."

Once Hawk was out of earshot, Douglas turned to him with a serious expression.

"You're sure about this—?"

"I'm sure, Bill. I want to help." *Let me redeem myself.*

Douglas held out his hand. "If I haven't heard from you in a few days, I'll head up there and bust you out of Bedlam."

Gregory laughed, thinking of the old Bethlem Royal, a psychiatric hospital in London whose nickname 'Bedlam' had inspired an entirely new word for 'chaos' and 'insanity'. Now, the hospital was one of the most revered psychiatric facilities in the world, but it had a long, sad history in its former incarnation as an asylum, providing the setting for some of the worst examples of inhumane treatment during the age of lunacy reform in the United Kingdom.

Nothing could be as bad as that.

Could it?

"Don't worry about me," he said. "I'm not going in there as a real patient, remember?"

Douglas gave him a searching look.

"Make sure you remember it too, Alex. You're not Michael anymore—you're only borrowing the name."

As the car pulled out of the car park a few minutes later, Douglas's last words replayed in Gregory's mind like a mantra.

You're Alex, not Michael.

Alex, not Michael.

If he repeated it often enough, he was sure to remember.

The journey from Quantico to the Catskill Mountains was a lengthy one.

They'd opted to make the eight-hour trip by road, and made a pit-stop every couple of hours at one of the greasy-spoon diners on the way to change driver. They spoke of Lorena, of profiling and of family and national pride, whilst steadfastly avoiding any talk of politics or religion until they lapsed into silence, wherein both men were content to enjoy the passing scenery.

When they reached Allentown, sixty-odd miles northwest of Philadelphia, they found a quiet corner where Hawk could put a call through to Buchanan Hospital. If their cover story was to be that Michael Jones had suffered a sudden and unexpected breakdown, it made sense not to give the hospital too much notice and so they'd decided to call a few hours ahead, but no more. This strategy carried the obvious risk of there being no rooms available, but it was a chance they were prepared to take.

Gregory listened as Hawk fell into the persona of a concerned cousin, setting out the various ways in which he, Michael, had suffered a mental lapse and needed somewhere private to recover. He felt the curious detachment of one who was peering through the looking-glass at the life he might have known, and at the man he might easily have been.

"They're expecting us this evening," Hawk said, ending the call. "You have a private doctor in New York, but he's away on vacation and you don't want to get into the State system, so you'd rather come straight to the Buchanan. I told them we couldn't provide any medical history because your notes are in the UK, your permanent place of residence. By the time they chase those up, you'll be out of there."

Gregory nodded, and steered the car back towards the freeway.

"Do you think they believed you?"

"No reason they shouldn't," Hawk replied, leaning back in his seat. "You mind if I catch some shuteye?"

It was only later, as they crossed the Pennsylvania border into New York, that Gregory realised Hawk had not answered his question.

CHAPTER 9

The Catskill Mountains were located in the south-eastern corner of New York State, west of the Hudson River. The peaks and waterfalls of the Catskills had been a draw for artists and musicians through the generations, and their proximity to the larger east coast cities attracted people looking to escape the metropolis and lose themselves in some thousands of acres of state parkland.

It was almost six o'clock by the time Gregory and Hawk reached the Roebling Bridge which, Hawk declared, was the oldest wire suspension bridge in the whole of the United States. Gregory was unsure whether that was intended to imply solid craftmanship or that the thing was liable to collapse at any moment. Either way, they crossed it, leaving behind the open farmland of Pennsylvania for the undulating forests of New York, travelling further away from the safety of the FBI's stronghold and deeper into the unknown.

A couple of hours later, they switched to Route 87, tracing the meandering line of the Hudson past quaint towns with hand-painted store fronts and clapboard walls, onward through miles of verdant green until they reached the turning marked, 'Woodstock'.

"It isn't far now," Hawk said.

Gregory raised a hand to shield his eyes from the setting sun, which blazed a fiery, amber red as it prepared to slip behind the line of trees and off the edge of the world.

"Have you been up here before?" he asked.

"You mean, with the FBI?"

"Either."

Hawk gave a light shrug. "Yeah, a few times. My mom loved that movie *Dirty Dancing*, which is supposed to be set up here, right? For a couple of summers, we all carted over from Delaware and went horseback riding and whatever the hell, while she tried to carry a freakin' watermelon for Patrick Swayze."

"And did she?"

"What?"

"Find a watermelon."

Hawk gave a funny half-laugh. "Yeah, there were a couple that holiday. Took a few more years until my Dad found out."

The sun bounced off his gunmetal aviators, blinding Gregory temporarily so he couldn't see the man's eyes, but he didn't really need to. Their respective professions had a reputation for attracting men and women with unresolved issues themselves; for his part, Gregory had long ago admitted his own motivations for entering the world of clinical psychology but, as a behavioural psychologist and an FBI agent, he wondered whether Agent Hawk had done the same.

"This is Woodstock," Hawk said, changing the subject. "The Buchanan's about eight miles north of here, up on Overlook Mountain. Do you want to make a stop?"

Gregory realised this would be his final opportunity to change his mind, if he wished to.

"Keep going," he said. "We've come this far—we may as well continue."

They passed through the town and followed the road north, winding their way up Overlook Mountain. Night was falling rapidly now, and with so much vegetation thereabouts, they could see very little of their surroundings except the twin beams of their headlights illuminating the road ahead. Up and up they climbed, passing unmarked roads that seemed to lead nowhere, until Hawk reduced his speed and consulted the GPS navigation on his dashboard.

"Signal's gone," he muttered. "The entrance should be around here, somewhere—"

"There," Gregory said, indicating a turning on the next bend. "Is that it?"

They saw a set of imposing, pillared gates with ornate ironwork.

"Must be," Hawk agreed. "You ready?"

Gregory nodded, and prepared to become Michael, one last time.

After a brief exchange with a disembodied voice, the gates swung open to reveal a long, single-track driveway flanked by forest on either side, where the trees were old and had grown tall, obliterating the last light of day. There was a curious stillness to the place, Gregory thought; no wind moved through the branches and no woodland creatures stirred in the brush. It was as though they'd fallen into one of Thomas Cole's romantic oil paintings—beautiful, but far removed from real life.

Presently, they emerged from the trees onto a wide ridge of parkland and big, open skies. A cloud passed over the moon but, as they drove on, it shifted suddenly to reveal Buchanan Hospital in all its glory. The hospital had been open since the turn of the twentieth century, but the house was much older, dating back to the Victorian era, when many of the larger mansion houses had been built following an industrial boom. Back then, it was known as 'Buchanan Manor' and belonged to a wealthy merchant of the same name, who'd prospered on the streets of New York and decided to build himself a summer house to prove it.

The house itself might have been described as a perfect pairing of Man and Nature. It ran over four stories in the Gothic style, with a clock tower and gables, and was situated on the edge of the ridge, so it appeared to overhang the mountainside. Immaculate lawned gardens swept out in terraces across the even ground around it, no doubt boasting panoramic views in daylight—the lawn giving way to a dip on the far side so that the stone wall marking the perimeter didn't appear as high as it was up close.

Hawk let out a long whistle.

"Pretty sweet digs," he said. "Looks more like a hotel than a psychiatric hospital."

"It's what people are paying for," Gregory said, and thought of the stark contrast between the world he would be entering, compared with the one he'd left back home in England.

Unlike the Arcadian scene he and agent Hawk where presently enjoying, patients at Southmoor were treated to a limited view of the hospital grounds, which were laid to lawn and mostly flat with concrete walkways for easy maintenance. Wooden benches had been set out, from which a patient could sit and look at the high perimeter wall that was protected by several layers of barbed wire, flood-lighting and numerous CCTV cameras positioned to capture every possible escape route they'd care to try. Much like the Buchanan, the hospital had been built during the Victorian era and it, too, had a clock tower. However, it had not started life as a rich man's country house; Southmoor had been purpose-built in the late 1800s as a lunatic asylum for the criminally insane and had remained true to that mission, albeit now employing a more humane approach to treatment than might have been the case at its inception. Now, it was one of a handful of high-security psychiatric hospitals in the United Kingdom, and home to some of the most infamous and disturbed individuals that country had to offer. Thanks to its chequered history and famous alumni, the hospital had garnered something of a reputation over the years and, in that regard, Gregory supposed the two hospitals had something in common.

That seemed to be where the similarities ended.

Patients at Southmoor did not herald from exclusively wealthy backgrounds, or have access to premium insurance; indeed, the opposite was more often the case, for its doors were open to all. In any event, Gregory had always found psychiatric illness to be a great leveller, free from any prejudice as to status, age, race, sexuality or gender. Some of his patients had spoken of how refreshing it was to at last feel 'at home' in the world, where their crimes and behaviours did not set them apart from their peers—chances were, theirs were less serious than the person seated beside them in the dining hall. On the other hand, his colleagues had spoken of how easy it could be to forget the differences between their patients, which was a dangerous problem to have. The moment a clinician forgot their case histories, they forgot just what their patients were capable of and why they were being treated in such a specialist facility. That made the therapists, psychologists and psychiatrists who worked at Southmoor susceptible to manipulation.

Gregory thought about all this as they drove up to the entrance, which looked warm and inviting with its whimsical columns and stained glass.

Appearances could so often be deceptive.

Hawk turned off the engine and turned to cast a critical eye over Gregory.

"We've gone over everything, but you've got my number if you need it. You going in looking like that?" he asked.

"Not everybody who's suffered a breakdown walks around foaming at the mouth," Gregory replied. "Leave the details to me."

He did, however, make one small concession by taking a moment to mismatch the buttons on his shirt. His general air of exhaustion came as standard.

"Ready, Michael?"

Gregory felt something stir inside him, and realised it was foreboding.

"Showtime," he muttered.

CHAPTER 10

For much of his life, Gregory had felt like an impostor.

First, entering the happy homes of surrogate families as a foster child, and later, as a man, walking through the corridors of Southmoor pretending to understand what normality felt like, or claiming to know how the criminal mind worked. It was therefore no great leap for him to step into the character of Michael Jones, having prepared for the role his whole life. Nonetheless, he felt a traitor to his own profession, and it was only by remembering he was playing a part to benefit the greater good that he was able to alleviate some of the guilt which gnawed at his belly.

There were no convicted offenders resident at Buchanan Hospital—or, at least, none they claimed to be aware of. Consequently, there was no need to enforce a prison-level admissions process, particularly as Michael Jones came of his own accord and without any history of suicidal behaviour, which put him firmly in the 'low-risk' category. Forms were completed, pockets and suitcase emptied of any illegal substances or personal effects that might conceivably be used as a weapon—or that somebody else could put to such use. This was standard practice, and gave Gregory no cause for alarm.

He handed his mobile phone to Hawk, and told him to take care of it.

Afterwards, they were greeted by the Hospital Administrator, a man of around forty, with a healthy tan and an over-bright smile.

"Mr Jones? We're so glad you could come and visit us," the Administrator said. "I'm Doctor Carl Kaufmann, the Administrator here at the Buchanan. May I take this opportunity to welcome you, and express our hope that you'll have a very healthy and happy stay with us."

Gregory opened his mouth to utter some polite response or other, but stopped himself just in time. People in the throes of a psychiatric break did not always remember how to converse politely, their minds being otherwise engaged by more troubling or intrusive thoughts.

He opted to remain silent, and distracted.

"Well," Kaufmann said, watching him closely. "If you'd like to follow me, we'll get you settled in. This might be a good time to say goodbye to your cousin—at least, for the time being."

Hawk put on a good show, and when he pulled Gregory in for an embrace he looked at him with eyes full of such concern, he might almost have believed their deception was true.

"Doctor Kaufmann says residents can call home between four and six, most days," Hawk said. "You'll remember to call me, to let me know how you're feeling?"

Gregory affected an air of agitation.

"Are you sure—am I doing the right thing?"

"*Absolutely*," Kaufmann said, reassuringly, before Hawk had a chance to reply. "Not merely the right thing, but the very *best* thing for your wellbeing, Michael."

"Don't worry about a thing," Hawk added. "Take care of yourself, Mikey."

Gregory raised a discreet eyebrow at the nickname. "Don't forget about me," he said, and his eyes held a warning.

The interior of Buchanan Hospital bore no resemblance to any mental health facility Gregory had ever visited before. In the first place, there were no electronic security doors fitted on the ground floor that he could see, and there was none of the usual rubber-coated flooring and pastel-painted walls he'd grown used to at Southmoor. Someone, sometime, had suggested that pale pinks and blues worked miracles for the disordered mind, leading to a boom in the bulk purchasing of said colours throughout the UK. Clearly, infantilising their patients was not part of the Buchanan's approach, for they'd chosen to retain much of the Manor's original features. The effect was to create a hospital setting that was more like a country club, and he half-expected to see patients gathered around a roaring fire, supping tumblers of whiskey while they talked about the progress they'd made that day.

It seemed too good to be true.

Gregory was led through the main hallway, which featured an enormous nineteenth-century painting of the old manor house by, he presumed, one of the original masters of the Hudson River Art Movement. All things being equal, he might have asked about it, but he was not supposed to be 'equal'. He was Michael Jones, who was not in any fit state to be conducting lengthy conversations around the history of art.

"We'll give you a full tour in the morning," Kaufmann said. "But, to give you a lay of the land, on the ground floor here, we have a number of private therapy rooms. There's also a fully-stocked library, a common room with some games and a television, as well as the main dining room, where we encourage our residents to eat together."

Gregory's ears pricked up at the mention of a library, but he banked down his enthusiasm for the present.

"Breakfast is between seven and ten, lunch is between twelve and two, and dinner is at seven," Kaufmann continued. "There are some other communal rooms we use for the occasional party, and to run group sessions. We have an art therapy class tomorrow afternoon, if you'd like to join in."

Gregory's first thought was that the patients who spent time at Buchanan Hospital were clearly afforded the best aesthetic environment in which to recover, and there seemed to be no shortage of alternative therapy classes, judging by the schedule Kaufmann was rattling off.

His second thought was to wonder about the other 99% of people for whom that kind of privilege would never be available. For years, he had lobbied the Hospital Board to run more frequent art, music and physical therapy sessions for the patients at Southmoor, having already gathered the evidence to show that there was a positive effect to be had on their overall behaviour. However, those sorts of questions always came down to money, and as a state-funded entity, there was never quite enough of it. Added to which, the provision of enhanced therapy sessions to violent criminal offenders was not popular amongst the general voting public, which was why prisons and special hospitals like Southmoor were bursting at the seams; nobody really wanted to hear about the improvements made to a deviant mind. People wanted *retribution*, not rehabilitation, and it made no difference how many times the research showed that intervention could lead to a drop in reoffending—no political party was brave enough to make such an unpopular move.

"I understand you've been living in Manhattan," Kaufmann said. "Before I took up the position here at the Buchanan, I used to have my practice on the Upper East Side, not far from the Metropolitan Museum of Art. I saw you admiring our painting, there—are you interested in art, Michael?"

Gregory realised he would have to be much more guarded, in future. He'd grown used to being the one to listen and observe the behaviour of others but he must remember that, for the next few days, he would be on the receiving end of that scrutiny.

It would be something of a novelty.

When he realised Kaufmann was still awaiting a response, Gregory affected a tired monotone he'd heard many of his patients use before, when suffering in the throes of depression or anxiety.

"Derivative," he muttered.

Kaufmann's demeanour remained relaxed and accommodating.

"Well," he said. "Perhaps you and I can talk more when you've had some time to rest. As they say, tomorrow is a new day. Come with me, and I'll show you to your room—you'll be staying on the first floor, in what we like to call our 'Hudson Wing.'"

Gregory would have liked to know what other wings there were at the Buchanan, but he cautioned himself against appearing too interested. A man who was unable to function normally in his everyday life had no business asking questions about staffing, funding and therapeutic approaches. A man like that would be quiet and withdrawn, his body past the point of physical exhaustion and his mind badly in need of repair.

As they mounted the wide oak staircase, he caught sight of one such man reflected in the long windows on the half-landing, pale as a ghost and no longer athletic, but thin.

He hardly recognised himself.

"This way, Michael."

CHAPTER 11

For the first time in a long while, Gregory slept soundly for eight solid hours.

Awakening to find himself bathed in sunlight was something akin to being reborn and, when he opened his eyes without the usual feeling of grogginess he'd come to expect, he felt an embarrassing urge to cry, or else sing a show tune from *Oklahoma!* in celebration of a beautiful morning.

In the end, he did neither, and swung his legs off the bed to view his surroundings with fresh, well-rested eyes. He was struck, once again, by the careful thought that had obviously been put into creating a 'home-from-home' atmosphere for the hospital's patrons. It was a nice touch, but they could have shoved him in an attic with bare floorboards and no heating, and he'd have been happy so long as he could enjoy the view.

With a nod to their health and safety obligations, the hospital had installed safety bars to the upper windows, but they did not detract from the uninterrupted panorama of the Hudson River Valley, the Ashokan Reservoir, and what Agent Hawk had called the 'Devil's Path' spreading out in a patchwork of misty greens and blues, for as far as the eye could see. Gregory might have been content to remain by his window watching the changing light across the valley but, at that moment, there came a knock at the door.

Another small concession to safety was the addition of porthole-sized Perspex windows, which had been inserted into the bedroom doors to allow the clinical staff to check on their patients without disturbing their sleep. Gregory had completed this task many times himself, during his rounds of the High Dependency Unit at Southmoor, but, as an intensely private man, he had never stopped to consider the impact of such an intrusive action on the patient's perception—even if the motive for looking was not voyeuristic.

The hospital had also taken the trouble to replace the old brass mechanisms on each of the doors with a high-tech electronic locking system, which meant that each bedroom could be accessed by the clinical staff using a master key card, which was kept on their person at all times. However, so long as safety was not compromised, these keys were to be used sparingly and a strong preference given to the personal autonomy of the hospital's residents—or so Dr Kaufmann had assured him the previous evening.

He almost called out a cheerful 'come in!' but caught himself just in time.

Instead, he walked to the door and opened it a crack.
"Yes?"

"Good morning!" the nurse trilled out. "I hope you slept well, Mr Jones. I see you're not dressed yet…"

Her sharp blue gaze catalogued his skinny frame beneath the lounge pants and t-shirt he wore, swept over his hair which, he admitted, was badly in need of a cut, and eventually came back to his face, which bore a genuine look of irritation thanks to her none-too-subtle inspection.

"You wouldn't want to miss breakfast," she said, in a tinkling tone of voice that grated on his nerves. "Why don't you have a nice shower, brush your teeth and hair, and find something comfortable to wear. Do you think you can do that for me?"

Gregory's instinctive reaction was to throw back some caustic remark about having been able to do it for the past thirty-something years, before he remembered that, for a person going through a breakdown, even those simple tasks could seem too much.

It put a different complexion on things.

"I'll manage," he said.

"Great! I'll come back in about fifteen minutes to show you where the dining room is," she promised.

The nurse, whose name turned out to be Tilda, was true to her word.

Precisely fifteen minutes later, she reappeared at his door to escort him downstairs. Gregory was conscious that he could not be seen to make *too* miraculous a recovery, before at least having had the opportunity to find out whether Lorena Romano occupied one of the other bedrooms at the hospital. He therefore kept up his quiet façade, which seemed consistent with a man struggling with his own demons. He was entirely unaware that this attempt to portray social withdrawal was not so very different from his usual, slightly misanthropic nature, and Douglas might have taken great pleasure in pointing out the irony, had he been there to see it. Tilda, at least, seemed unconcerned by his lack of conversation, and continued to chatter about this and that as they made their way down to the ground floor.

The old manor house was even more impressive in the light of day, its grandeur not having been allowed to fade too badly with the passage of time. Perhaps the general warmth of their surroundings and the beauty of the landscape managed to produce a calming effect because, unlike other facilities where it was normal to overhear the occasional sob or cry from a person in distress, as they moved through the long, panelled corridors in search of breakfast, the only other sound that could be heard was the thrum of conversation coming from the dining room and the sound of a radio or a television somewhere not far away.

The dining room was one of the larger reception rooms from the original manor, and the hospital had retained it for the same use, evidently continuing their desire to treat their residents like paying guests at a five-star hotel. There was something to be said for this approach, Gregory thought, judging by the orderly way those residents appeared to be enjoying their first meal of the day. At Southmoor, it was not unusual for patients to reject food, or use it as a means of controlling at least one part of their lives, when so much else seemed unmanageable. However, he wondered whether that would still be the case if the food was half as appetising as that currently gracing the plates at the Buchanan.

"This is the dining room," Tilda said, unafraid to state the obvious. "Let's find you a seat and make some introductions, hmm?"

Eight tables had been arranged around the room, with four chairs apiece. Some were fully occupied, others had only two or three people—including a nurse, in some cases— and one table stood empty. Gregory made a quick sweep of all of them, studying the faces of the men and women gathered around. There was an even split of genders and, as he would later learn, the male and female patients were entitled to use the same common areas but spent their nights in separate wings of the house, each requiring a different manner of key card entry.

The proprieties must be observed, after all.

He recalled the image of Lorena Romano to the front of his mind and searched the room again, without success.

She wasn't there.

"—Michael?"

He realised Tilda had been speaking to him, and now appeared to be awaiting some response from him.

"Sorry, what did you say?" he asked.

As she looked into his sad green eyes, she felt a maternal tug for the young man who seemed so lost. Speaking very slowly, she repeated her question.

"I was asking whether you feel up to meeting anybody, or whether you'd rather sit with me and have a quiet breakfast?"

He wasn't sure whether 'quiet' and 'Tilda' were likely to be consistent in that context, but he was willing to run the risk. He had no particular desire to make friends with any of the other residents and he was more likely to extract information about the running of the hospital from one of its nurses.

"A quiet breakfast sounds good," he said.

CHAPTER 12

There were many things that could be learned from Tilda, if one had even a passing interest in horticulture or soap operas—or advanced interrogation techniques, judging by her superlative ability to avoid discussion of any topics remotely concerning the operational running of Buchanan Hospital. The only information she had been willing to share on that score was that Gregory—or, rather, Michael Jones—was one of twenty-three current residents.

Gregory had counted nineteen other diners at breakfast, not counting himself and Tilda, or the two other nurses he'd spotted in the room. That left three residents still unaccounted for, whether because they'd enjoyed an earlier breakfast, or had been absent for some other reason. Although not sprawling, the hospital was large enough to present a challenge for him to track down the missing three, especially since individual treatment plans were not shared with fellow patients, for obvious reasons, and not all the residents may be well enough to join in at mealtimes.

Still, he was not disheartened at having struck out on the first attempt, and resolved to take every opportunity to mingle with the other residents, to see if that might throw up any leads.

However, immediate progress in the search for Lorena was thwarted by the small matter of his own 'treatment'. After breakfast, when he might have liked to check the other common areas on the ground floor or take a stroll around the grounds, he was prevented from doing so by Tilda's cheerful edict that he was to meet with Doctor Palmer, who would be his therapist. The novelty of his situation hadn't yet worn off, and Gregory told himself to go through the motions of an assessment, remembering all the while that it related to Michael Jones and not to Alexander Gregory.

The first clear thought to enter Gregory's mind when he walked into Dr Palmer's office was, *wow*.

The room was filled with light, streaming in from the windows which made up two of its four walls and looked out across what, at first glance, appeared to be nothing but blue sky.

"Lovely, isn't it?

Gregory turned to find a woman watching him from the edge of the room, where she'd been returning a book to its shelf.

"I'm surprised you manage to get any work done," he said, and could have bitten his tongue off.

Michael, not Alexander, remember?

"Thank you, Tilda. Perhaps you could come back for Mr Jones in an hour?"

Once they were alone, Dr Palmer moved across to where a sofa and two easy chairs had been arranged at one end of the room.

"I thought we could have some tea or coffee while we get to know one another," she said. "Why don't you come and sit down?"

She gestured him to the sofa while she moved to one of the chairs, keeping a professional distance between them. Alexander Gregory fully approved of her approach, and yet Michael Jones found himself oddly bereft. He didn't stop to analyse his own thought processes, but did as he was asked, taking a seat on the worn leather chesterfield.

"May I call you Michael, or would you rather I call you Mr Jones?" she asked.

He was impressed by her quick approach to boundary-setting, and the smooth manner in which she did it.

"Michael's fine," he said.

She smiled, just a quick upward turn of the lips, but he caught it. He wondered why he felt compelled to make her smile again.

"Thank you. You can call me Naomi or Doctor Palmer, whichever you prefer. What can I get you, Michael—some tea? Or would you prefer coffee?"

"Black coffee, please."

They went through a cordial dance, while each took the opportunity to make a brief survey of the other, then Palmer reached for her notebook and a pen.

"If you don't mind, Michael, I'm going to take some notes. It helps me to remember the important things you tell me, so that I won't forget by the time our next session comes around. It also helps me to think about the ways I might be able to help, and to make sure I don't get it wrong. Is that alright with you?"

He nodded, beginning to realise he'd stumbled onto very dangerous ground. He'd have been less than human if he failed to admit the good doctor was a very attractive woman; even now, the sun burnished her chestnut hair so it gleamed around her face, which was a perfect oval offset by a pair of big brown eyes.

But that was just window dressing.

He hadn't missed the framed certificates hanging on the wall from several well-known universities around the United States, nor the sharp, thorough way she'd put her new patient at ease. There was nothing quite as devastating as an intelligent woman, especially one with the face of a Madonna.

Which elicited the second clear thought he'd had, since entering her office.

Shit.

"So, Michael. Would you like to tell me why you're here?"

To see if the wife of a notorious Mafia boss is one of your patients, he thought. *To see if Buchanan Hospital is controlled by the Romano family, and if so, whether it's been accepting bribes to do away with difficult or undesirable people. In short, Doctor Palmer, I'm here to find out if you're all that you seem to be.*

"I had a breakdown," he said.

"How do you know?"

It was a good question to ask. Gregory knew that the term 'nervous breakdown' was not used in the medical community to describe any one illness. However, there were all manner of other symptoms and illnesses related to it, and he could have recited chapter and verse about all of them.

For now, he selected a few that sprang to mind.

"Ah…I've been feeling a lot of stress and anxiety," he said. "Insomnia, dizzy spells, trembling hands, hallucinations, night terrors…"

Gregory trailed off, realising that it had taken no effort at all to describe those symptoms, all of which he genuinely suffered on a regular basis.

"Anything else?" she asked, making rapid notes on her pad.

He cleared his throat, and decided he might as well go all-in.

"The occasional panic attack," he said. "Chest pain, shortness of breath, that sort of thing."

"When's the last time you had one?"

Last night.

"A couple of days ago," he said.

90

"How about...low thoughts? Have you considered suicide?"

He shook his head.

"No," he lied. *Not for a very long time, at least.*

The wonderful thing about helping others, whose pain was often so much greater than his own, had been in discovering how fragile and precious life was. Even one you hadn't asked for nor wished for—nor been able to control, at times.

There was always *hope*.

Palmer set the notepad aside and walked over to her desk, where she retrieved a sphygmomanometer, a word he'd always struggled to pronounce, and so preferred to call a 'blood-pressure meter'. It consisted of an inflatable cuff which acted to collapse and then release the artery under the cuff in a controlled way, and a mercury manometer which measured the pressure.

"Unfortunately, we don't have access to your previous medical records," she said. "That being the case, would you mind if I take a measurement of your blood pressure?"

To do that, she needed to move closer, and came to sit beside him on the sofa. She unfolded the machine and then looked at his attire with—he thought—a touch of embarrassment.

"Ah, I'm not sure—can you roll your sleeve up to the bicep?"

He tried, but the slim-fitting sweater didn't make it that far.

"I'm afraid I'll have to ask you to take it off, for a moment."

Gregory said nothing, but removed the sweater in one smooth motion and then held out his arm.

She busied herself fitting the cuff, the pads of her fingers brushing his skin as she hooked it around his arm, and then she pressed a button to begin the process.

There was a heavy silence as the machine did its work, where they did not look at one another.

Then, the machine gave a long *beep*.

"Ninety over sixty," she said. "That's very good."

She unravelled the machine and moved away quickly, keeping her back to him as he pulled the sweater back over his head.

"Often, people going through a breakdown suffer from raised blood pressure," she said, returning to her seat.

Was it his imagination, or did her colour seem a little higher than before?

It was a warm room, he supposed.

"Tell me all about yourself, Michael," she said, picking up her pen.

He ran a hand through his hair, not knowing where to begin or how much to say. What had started as a novel exercise and, perhaps, a challenge against his own profession, was fast becoming an unexpected and unwanted intrusion into his own psyche. He couldn't speak of Michael's feelings without drawing on his own, or invent Michael's past history without being reminded of his own, either. He needed to remember why he was there, and stay focused; not be taken in by a woman's soft voice, or the cossetted feeling of safety inside her sunny office.

A gilded cage was still a cage, after all.

CHAPTER 13

After his session with Dr Palmer, Tilda arrived with characteristic promptness to continue his guided tour of the hospital before lunch.

It consisted of two wings—one for men and another for women—each separated into two wards, one for residents who had been assessed as 'low-risk' and another for those assessed as 'high-risk'. His own bedroom was located on the 'low-risk' corridor of Hudson Wing, so named because the views from each of the bedrooms on that side of the house looked out across the valley, towards the river. The Overlook Wing housed the female residents and had been named for the mountain upon which the house was built.

Gregory hadn't been able to locate an access to Overlook Wing, or undertake a full recce of the hospital's security arrangements, and Tilda was unforthcoming on either of those subjects. For her, the tour was an opportunity to introduce Michael to some of his fellow residents, having apparently decided he needed all the help he could get in that department. She paraded him through the common room first, where two male residents were engaged in a serious game of table football, whilst a female resident lounged in a high-backed chair beside the fireplace reading a tattered paperback. The fire, he saw, was for decorative purposes only, but it was enough to give the impression of being somewhere other than a registered psychiatric hospital. One of the duty nurses remained in the room to supervise at all times, and was seated by the door.

"Good morning everyone," Tilda said. "I'd like to introduce you to a new resident. This is Michael, and he'll be staying with us for a little while."

When nobody reacted, not even to give him a cursory glance, she let out one of her tinkling laughs.

"I guess everybody's caught up in their own activities," she said. "Over there playing table football we've got Harry and Marco, who've been with us a while now. They ought to be able to show you where everything is."

Gregory looked at the two men and thought that they were not so much caught up in their game as unwilling to engage with the nursing staff. Both were men in their fifties, each dressed in baggy jogging pants and tee-shirts. Both wore thick beards and, because it was fashionable at the time, he imagined that made it harder for the nursing staff to know whether it was a sign of personal neglect, or a statement of identity.

"That's Rosie, in the corner there," Tilda said. "How's that book coming along?"

Rosie was a woman of around sixty, comfortably rounded with a mop of steel-grey hair which fell in soft ringlets around her face. Her hair reminded Gregory of one of the old porcelain dolls his mother used to collect, with their fixed, painted faces and tightly-packed hair; so much so, he wondered if it was real.

She looked up that time, and squinted towards the door.

"The Duke of Warwickshire is about to burst into the church and reclaim Marion," she said, in a strong Midwestern drawl.

"What's the book called?" Gregory wondered aloud. From where he stood, he could see only an outline of two scantily-clad people dressed in period costume.

"*Lady Marion and the Duke,*" she said. "Have you read it?"

Gregory shook his head. "Not yet," he replied, gravely.

"You can borrow it, when I'm finished," Rosie said. "But I need it back, otherwise he'll be unhappy."

"Who will?"

"The Duke, of course."

By the time lunchtime came around, there was still no sign of Lorena Romano.

He met a number of other residents, ranging from young, angsty men and women suffering from depressive disorders or addictions, to older men and women with the same maladies but longer memories—and then there was Kitty.

Kitty had been born Catherine Marie Vanderkamp, the only grandchild of a shipping magnate who'd made his fortune at around the same time old Buchanan made his. Too young to have lived through the Great Depression, she nonetheless remembered its repercussions, having witnessed her father's slow decline over the years that followed. Hers had been a privileged life beset by personal tragedies, including the loss of not only her father, but her brother, husband and child, all of whom had died in a devastating fire which ravaged their mansion in the Hamptons forty years ago. Now, she was a woman of eight-five with a severely impaired memory, and a penchant for leopard print, sherry in the afternoons and *Tom and Jerry* cartoons.

In the time Gregory had spent sitting with her in one of the sitting rooms, she'd repeated the same story at least three times and had forgotten his name each time he told her.

"Are you married, dear?" she asked him, for the second or third time. "I'm married, you know. Just up here to take the air. My Terrence will be back here, any day now, to take me home again."

Gregory only smiled.

From their short acquaintance, it seemed to him that Kitty had built up an elaborate fiction; a new reality she found preferable to the truth. It wasn't unusual—people re-wrote events and conversations all the time, often re-casting themselves in a more positive light. It was a coping mechanism of sorts but, in Kitty's case, she had taken things to the extreme.

"Come on now, Mrs Steenberg," Tilda said. "It is about time for some lunch, wouldn't you say?"

"Well, I don't know—shouldn't we wait for Terrence?"

"Oh, he'll be right along," Tilda said. "Why don't we ask this nice young man to take your arm?"

Gregory was happy to oblige. He'd spent a pleasant hour listening to her stories of a time he'd never know, imagining New York in the days when the United Nations building had been built, before men like Cary Grant made it famous in *North by Northwest*. They'd watched cartoons while Tilda sat quietly watching them both, and he hadn't minded that, either.

He held out the crook of his arm.

"It would be my pleasure, Mrs Steenberg. Maybe you can tell me about the time you joined the Women's March through Central Park?"

"Oh, now, that was fun…what was your name again, honey?"

"Michael," he said, patiently.

She stopped dead and peered at him with old, myopic eyes.

"Doesn't suit you," she declared. "You seem more like an 'Andrew', or an 'Alexander'…maybe a 'Ryan'?"

He let out a short bark of laughter and thought that, while she may be a little old and delusional, she certainly was not blind.

"All the Ryans I know are better men than me," he said. "I'll stick with Michael—for now."

CHAPTER 14

Shortly after four, Gregory appealed to the omnipresent Tilda to show him where he might ring his cousin, who would surely be worrying about him. Encouraged by the display of familial feeling, she led him to one of several small sitting rooms located near the main entrance, which had been set up as comfortable spaces in which residents could make a phone call—under supervision, of course.

He feigned an embarrassing moment where he was unable to recall Hawk's mobile phone number, passing it off as 'another of those short-term memory blips' he'd been having so often, lately. Tilda had made a comforting sound in the back of her throat and agreed to go and look the number up in the filing room, if he agreed not to do anything *silly*.

Having made a solemn promise, Gregory wasted no time in dialling the number as soon as she left, which was answered on the first ring.

"How's it going, cuz?"

"Slow progress," Gregory said, ever mindful of the possibility that the line may be tapped. "But I'll keep going."

"That's the spirit," Hawk said. "Have you made any new...friends?"

"A couple," Gregory said, and made a sheepish face as Tilda bustled back into the room, as if to say he'd remembered the number, after all.

She flapped a piece of paper at him in mock anger, then settled herself on a chair to read a glossy magazine.

"It seems a nice place," he said, and caught Tilda's smile. Apparently, she could read about a forthcoming episode of *The Young and the Restless* and still keep an ear open to listen in on his conversation.

Multi-tasking at its best.

"Oh yeah?" Hawk said. "What about the doctors—they treating you well?"

"Seem to be," Gregory said. "Dr Palmer says my blood pressure is normal, and she thinks talking therapies are a good place to start. If that doesn't work, she'll look at meds."

"How big is the place?" Hawk asked, keeping his tone light, consistent with that of a concerned relative. "See anybody you know?"

"It's pretty small," Gregory said, keeping an eye on Tilda's bent head. "There is a mix of men and women, and everybody seems friendly enough. I don't see any of our family members, if that's what you mean."

He heard Hawk sigh, and was sorry he didn't have better news to impart.

"So what's the plan for tomorrow? You going to head along to one of those yoga classes I saw advertised on the website?"

"Actually, there's a group therapy session tomorrow morning. Dr Palmer thinks it is a good idea for me to go," he said, making sure to mention the name of his therapist so Hawk could run a check on her, if he hadn't already. "Everybody goes along, together."

"Sounds great," Hawk agreed. "Why don't you call me tomorrow and let me know how it went?"

Shortly after, Gregory ended the call, feeling relieved at having spoken to someone who knew who he really was.

Then, as Tilda continued to flick through the pages of her magazine, he keyed in the second number he'd memorised, and clutched the receiver in his hand while it began to ring.

But there was no answer.

Gregory gave up after the second attempt, reasoning that Bill Douglas could be driving or otherwise unable to pick up the phone—perhaps Hawk hadn't told him of the designated times.

And still, he felt the first real stirrings of worry.

Paranoia, he told himself.

Places like these did funny things to your head.

Gregory was re-energised about the mission following his phone call to Agent Hawk, but there still remained the problem of not having seen Lorena Romano. She had been absent at breakfast and lunch, there had been no sign of her in any of the common areas throughout the day, and she hadn't opted to take part in the art therapy class earlier in the afternoon, where he'd had been obliged to produce a charcoal drawing of a vase of flowers—a creation which he had to acknowledge was not fit to grace the walls of Buchanan Hospital.

It was concerning that he hadn't been able to reach Bill Douglas. Though it was somewhat lowering to admit, the man was his only real friend in the world and the only person he could bear to spend any amount of time with. His first day as an in-patient at the Buchanan had been an unsettling experience, not least because he doubted his own ability to keep up the fiction without sacrificing something of his own mental wellbeing along the way, and he'd looked forward to hearing a friendly voice to remind him that someone out there believed in him.

With these troubling thoughts circling his mind, Gregory followed Tilda back into the main corridor, where he almost ran into a man heading in the opposite direction.

"Sorry," he muttered.

When he stepped back, his heart gave one hard thump against the wall of his chest.

The man was Paolo Romano.

CHAPTER 15

Coming face to face with one of the most powerful and dangerous men in America reminded Gregory of an old saying about dogs and snakes. When a dog had done wrong, it looked away—but when a snake had done wrong, it looked you right in the eye.

As he looked into the dark, beady eyes of Paolo Romano, he knew he looked into the eyes of a snake.

Time seemed to pause as they faced one another, and Gregory had the impression of being sized-up—as though Romano was comparing his face with all the others he'd known, and struggling to make it fit.

"Watch where you're goin," he said eventually.

His voice was heavily-accented and slightly nasal, as though he were suffering from a persistent cold—or, indeed, a persistent case of insufflation.

He turned to the nurse, who hovered nearby.

"How you doin', Tilda?"

"Oh, just fine, Mr Romano," she gushed. "Thank you for asking."

He turned back to Gregory. "Who's this?" he asked.

The question might have been directed at Tilda, but it was Gregory who answered.

"I'm Michael," he said.

"That it?" Romano said. "Your father never give you a second name, or what?"

"Jones," Gregory said, and felt his stomach perform a slow flip.

There was no way he could have known he would bump into Lorena's husband but, now that he had, he knew there was no going back. A man like Romano didn't like new faces, especially ones he knew nothing about, but that wouldn't be the case for very long. He would probably instruct one of his goons to run a standard search on 'Michael Jones', as soon as he left the hospital.

He only hoped the FBI had been true to their word, and that the paper trail would stand up to scrutiny.

"There's a nice view from the garden," Romano said, conversationally, "but you gotta be careful you don't go too near the edge."

With that, Romano continued down the corridor towards the Administrator's Office, where Doctor Kaufmann was already waiting to greet him like a visiting monarch.

"Who was that? Gregory asked, once they'd disappeared.

Tilda was no longer wearing her trademark smile—in fact, she looked visibly shaken.

"Just—a visitor."

She steered him away.

Gregory hesitated, and was tempted to put another call through to Agent Hawk to update him, but it would look far too suspicious and, besides, he still hadn't seen Lorena in the flesh. There were many reasons her husband might be visiting—to identify a body, for instance—and none of them could be ruled out, yet.

"Come on," Tilda said. "I'll show you the grounds."

When Gregory joined the other residents for dinner, he caught his first sight of Lorena Romano.

He didn't spot her at first—he'd expected to find her seated at one of the tables with the others, but instead she moved amongst them, helping to dish out the food. She was small and slight, moving nimbly from table to table, her greying hair bundled into a loose bun atop her head.

She was, he realised, doing what she'd done for much of her adult life.

Serving others.

Finally seeing her alive and unharmed was like finding a rare butterfly previously thought to be extinct.

"Where would you like to sit?" Tilda asked him. "There's a spot over there, beside Harry and Marco—"

Gregory made a quick survey, trying to judge where Lorena might eventually settle. He spotted a couple of free seats beside Rosie—who had moved on to the next in her series of romantic novels—and thought that seemed the most likely.

But even as he opened his mouth to suggest it, another of the residents plonked themselves down and, to his chagrin, Lorena took up the last chair.

"Damn," he muttered.

"What's that?" Tilda gave him a considering look, no doubt making a mental note that he'd started talking to himself.

"Nothing," Gregory said, and walked over to where the other two men were engaged in a heated debate about baseball.

They fell silent as he and Tilda approached and, sensing her presence might be an impediment to their manly discussion, the nurse excused herself.

"I'll leave you three to get better acquainted," she said. "I'll be right over there, with the other nurses, so you just holler if you need me, Michael."

Gregory had a flash memory of his first day at school, when things hadn't been so bad at home. Closing his eyes, he could remember the feel of his mother's hand clutching his own as they'd walked across the playground, and her voice—not manic, then, but maternal—telling him she'd never be far away.

I'll never be far away.

His eyes flew open again, and his head jerked around at the sound of his mother's voice in his ear.

But, of course, she wasn't there.

It was a vivid sensory memory, that was all.

He scrubbed the palms of his hands against his legs to rid himself of the sensation and looked up to find the two other men staring openly at him.

"Boy, you're as crazy as the rest of us," Harry said, and let out a hooting laugh.

"Welcome to the Funny Farm, kid," Marco added, shoving another forkful of pasta into his mouth. "You can get out anytime you like, but nobody leaves."

"That's the wrong quote, you moron," Harry said, sending small drops of spittle onto his beard. "You gonna rip off *Hotel California,* at least get it right."

"I made it up, right then," Marco said.

"Bullshit," Harry replied, dragging a piece of garlic bread around his plate. "I never heard worse bullshit than the stuff that comes outta your mouth."

"Except when you're talkin' about the Yankees," Marco shot back.

Gregory listened to them for a while and thought that, in any other setting, they'd have been two regular guys chewing the fat.

"So, what're you in here for?" Harry asked, suddenly. "You try and jump off the Brooklyn Bridge or what?"

The question was delivered with such breathtaking nonchalance, Gregory was taken aback. In psychiatric circles—in *any* circles—suicide was no laughing matter, and to speak of it so lightly went against the grain.

"I had a nervous breakdown," he said.

"Ah, God, do you remember the days when a breakdown was all you had to worry about?" Harry asked his friend, and Marco let out a long, nostalgic sigh.

"Yeah, think I had my first one back in '88. Bad day on the stock market," he said, as an aside. "Second one around '95…I must be due another, by now."

Harry let out a wheezing laugh.

"What about you?" Gregory asked, while his gaze slipped over to watch Lorena, trying to gauge her mood from afar.

"They say I've got BPD," Harry said, referring to Borderline Personality Disorder.

"I say he's a grumpy sonofabitch," Marco said.

Harry let out another hooting laugh.

"And you?" Gregory asked.

Marco finished chewing his garlic bread, then dabbed his face with a napkin, delicate as you like. "Schizophrenia," he replied shortly.

"Yeah, they tell him he's thinkin' things that just ain't real, like the time he said the Mets would win next season."

That incited another long debate about players and tactics, and Gregory was content to watch their byplay. He looked around the room, listening to the quiet clatter and scrape of rounded, plastic cutlery on plates, and wondered how many of the people there had benefited from having company and a friendly ear, just as much as the medication and psychotherapy.

He looked over at Lorena Romano, who was talking with Rosie about her latest book, and thought that she needed that friendly ear more than most.

CHAPTER 16

The wall was high, and built of stone.

Paradise lay beyond it; a land of forests and rivers, of waterfalls and lakes so clear, he'd be able to see his reflection in their crystal waters.

He stretched out a hand to touch the wall, and felt it contract beneath his fingers, moving to the beat of his own heart. The grass was dry underfoot, and the sun warm against his skin; the scent of pine and wild garlic a pleasant balm to his senses.

He could have lived his whole life in that comfortable spot, if only he'd never seen what lay on the other side of that wall.

The skies shifted suddenly, and heavy storm clouds appeared, blotting out the sun.

In his sleep, Gregory's hands clutched the sheets of his bed to anchor himself in place, but he couldn't prevent the nightmare from taking a stranglehold.

He saw himself turn and look back at the house, with its pretty gables and window. The wind began to howl, whipping through the trees and rushing across the lawn to burn his skin.

There, it whispered. *Do you feel alive, now?*

All around, the air swirled with bark and leaves. Faster and faster it went, snagging his skin with a thousand tiny cuts as he tried to fight his way through the maelstrom, back to the house.

Michael!

Michael, come in now, it's dinnertime!

Above the sound of the wind, he heard a woman's voice calling to him. He tried to raise his head to look for her, but the force of the wind was so strong, it drove him to his knees. Tears ran from his eyes, and he threw up an arm to shield himself.

Michael!

Through the blurred haze of wind and rubble, he thought he saw a woman standing on the terrace. The house was different from before, and no longer stood in the shadow of a mountain, but in the middle of a large garden. It was tall and red-bricked, with ivy growing along one side, and a climbing frame on the lawn, its swings blowing wildly in the wind before coming loose from its concrete foundations, rising up to join the cyclone roaring high above his head.

He tried again to move, crawling on his hands and knees towards the woman who held her arms open to him, sobbing in frustration as the wind drove him back, time and again.

He cried out, and with an almighty effort, propelled himself forward, hands tearing at the earth as he half-ran, half-crawled towards home.

Except, it was not his home.

The image shifted again as he drew near, and he saw tall towers, and windows with ornamental bars.

On the porch, there was a line of women waiting for him.

Madeleine, Kitty, Maggie, Tilda, Amy, Emma, Naomi, Lorena…

And standing in the centre of them all was Cathy Jones.

You can check out anytime you like, she said, and they all started to laugh, the sound of it mingling with the wind which pummelled his body and tormented his mind.

Gregory awoke to the sound of his own screams, and then Tilda's firm voice, telling him to stay calm.

"Michael, wake up! Wake up!"

He tried to move, but two other pairs of hands held him firm.

"Where—?"

"It's alright, honey," she said. "You were having a nightmare—and a bad one, by the sound of it."

As his mind made the slow journey back to consciousness, he remembered where he was, and why.

Buchanan Hospital.

He wanted to fight the hands that held him, to break free and return to his lonely flat in London to lick his wounds in private. He didn't want these strangers looking at him as though he were a specimen; something to be studied or even pitied.

But, that wouldn't have helped matters.

"I'm—I'm alright," he said, through parched lips. "I don't need—"

"Shh, okay, just relax. We're going to let go of your arms and legs now, alright?"

He let his body go limp.

Tilda watched him closely, then nodded towards the other nurses.

"I think we'll be okay now," she said. "Ingrid, could you get us some fresh water, please?"

When the other two left, Tilda reached across to flip on the night light, consisting of a single switch on the wall since no wires were allowed in any of the bedrooms.

"That's better," she said, reaching down to pick up the bedclothes he'd kicked onto the floor.

Then, she perched on the edge of the bed and reached for his wrist to take his pulse.

"Let's see how you're doing," she said.

Gregory lifted himself into a seated position and leaned back against the padded headboard, trying to let his mind go blank.

"Still racing a bit, but better than it was. How long have you been getting these night terrors, Michael?"

Gregory flinched at the name, and ran a tired hand over his face.

Thirty years, off and on.

"Just the last little while," he said.

Tilda sighed, feeling an inappropriate urge to ruffle his hair. Instead, she stood up and opened the shutters.

"Sun's rising," she said, looking out across the valley. "Why don't you go for a jog around the grounds, Michael? You might feel better, shaking off the cobwebs."

Gregory started to say 'no', but found himself nodding instead.

He'd stopped to buy a pair of cheap trainers in one of the markets he and Hawk had passed on their journey north, so he might as well break them in.

"I'll be back in time for breakfast," he said.

"You'd better be," she said. "I don't want to have to send out a search party."

Her last remark was delivered lightly, but it held a warning. Gregory knew that the policy for low-risk patients like himself was to encourage exercise and independence, so long as it remained safe to do so. He knew that, following his nightmare, she would be in two minds as to whether she should keep him under close surveillance or encourage him to work off the adrenaline.

"I'll come back," he said. "If only to find out what happens in next week's episode."

She smiled beautifully, and left him to get dressed.

CHAPTER 17

Group therapy sessions at the Buchanan were generally conducted by one of the psychiatrists at the hospital, of which there were usually three, including Doctor Palmer and Doctor Kaufmann, who had the additional honour of being the hospital's administrator. The third had been a man by the name of George Kellerman, until his departure a few months ago to take up a position elsewhere, and he had not yet been replaced.

The session that morning was led by Doctor Palmer, who had chosen to have it on a shaded area of the lawn so the residents might enjoy the benefits of sunshine and fresh air while they were discussing some of the difficulties in their lives. The nursing staff brought with them trays of fresh lemonade, ripe strawberries and, much to the general delight of those assembled, a large dish of fresh cannoli, filled with chocolate, lemon and pistachio cream.

"One of our other residents, Lorena, is an amazing cook," Tilda explained, as they walked across the lawn. "We try to encourage our residents to carry on doing the things that make them happy, and Lorena has quite a hand with desserts."

Gregory saw his chance.

"Actually, I enjoy cooking, too," he said.

It was not altogether a lie; he'd enjoyed cooking for others, on rare the occasions he'd ever invited anyone into his home.

"Would you like to join Lorena in the kitchen?" Tilda asked.

Gregory feigned surprise. "Well, if it wouldn't be an imposition—"

"Not at all," she said. "Let me speak to Doctor Palmer about it."

"Hello again, Alexander!"

Gregory's head whipped around in horror, but it was only Kitty, who'd taken the chair next to his own.

"No, no, Mrs Steenberg," Tilda said. "This is *Michael*."

Kitty looked confused.

Thankfully, there was no further opportunity to argue the point as Doctor Palmer took her seat and prepared to begin the session.

It was warm outside, and Gregory watched her shrug out of her blazer and hook it over the back of her chair. As she sat down, the plastic key card she normally kept on her waistband dug uncomfortably into her side, so she unclipped it and slid it inside the pocket of her blazer.

In that moment, he was reminded of an incident that had happened shortly after he'd first joined the clinical staff at Southmoor. One of his new patients was an old man who'd recently celebrated his eightieth birthday and who struggled to walk without a stick. He was awaiting an operation to remove cataracts from both of his eyes, and looked like a war veteran, or perhaps the kindly grandfather he'd once seen in an advert for Murray Mints.

Back in those days, Gregory had fallen into the unfortunate habit of tucking the unwieldy key chain he was forced to carry into the back pocket of his trousers when he was doing the rounds. On this particular occasion, he'd seen Arthur walking in the corridor on the way to the common room when suddenly he'd fallen.

Full of concern, Gregory had rushed over to help him back to his feet, and even accompanied him to the common room.

It had been a full five minutes before he realised the keys had been lifted, and it was only a combination of good fortune and Arthur's rheumatoid arthritis that had prevented the man from making good on his bid for freedom. Later, when he'd gone back over Arthur's file, Gregory had learned that before he'd murdered his wife and three children forty years before, Arthur had started life as a petty thief and pickpocket.

Even the arthritic hand could be quicker than the eye.

As he'd told his junior staff time and again, never assume anything when there are facts more readily to hand, and never let your guard down.

"Thank you all for joining me this morning," Dr Palmer said. "Before we get started, the first thing I'd like us all to do is take our shoes off. It's a beautiful day, today, and I think we should feel the grass between our toes, don't you?"

Evidently, this was not unheard of in Dr Palmer's group therapy sessions, and he watched the others kick off their shoes with gleeful abandon.

He followed suit, and had to admit it was a liberating sensation.

Glancing across at Kitty, he was amused to note that her toes had been polished in a leopard-print pattern, which happened to match the blouse she wore.

"There," Naomi said. "That's better, isn't it?"

She smiled at each of the faces in the group and, as her dark eyes passed over him, Gregory couldn't prevent a flicker of awareness, which he repressed.

Across the circle, Harry and Marco were seated together as usual, clutching handfuls of fresh cannoli which they stuffed into their bearded mouths as if they were popcorn. Some medications had the unfortunate side-effect of causing weight gain which, combined with a sweet tooth, could lead to all manner of physical ailments like heart disease. It was one of the saddest ironies of the job, he'd always thought, that in working so hard to protect a person's mind, the body was left to fall by the wayside.

Some of the other residents seated in the circle reminded Gregory of the patients he'd grown used to working with at Southmoor. Though he knew nothing of their individual case histories, statistically-speaking, he knew that a large proportion of the group would have suffered all manner of trauma in their lives—physical and psychological—that were visible and invisible to the naked eye. He could see that a couple of them wore their troubles on their sleeves, in behavioural tics or as a roadmap of lines on their careworn faces. Others showed the unmistakable markers of heavy sedation, which left their faces vacant of expression as they slumped in their chairs, staring into space.

Almost all of them shuffled or fidgeted in their chairs, with the marked exception of Lorena, who was seated with her hands linked on her lap looking entirely at ease.

"Now, I know most of you will be familiar with one another," she said. "But, we have a newcomer to our group today and I'd like you all to make him feel welcome."

She turned to look at Gregory again.

"Michael? Would you like to introduce yourself to the group?"

Gregory would have no problem with that, but Michael? He considered whether a man in the throes of a nervous breakdown would be up to it. He decided it was possible, but there would be outward signs of stress.

He did a bit of fidgeting himself, before speaking again.

"I—okay, I guess. I'm Michael," he said, in a deliberately stilted voice. "I'm thirty-seven, and I'm from London."

Doctor Palmer gave him an encouraging smile.

"Is there anything else you'd like to share?"

He fell silent, and shook his head, feeling all kinds of guilt about his flagrant malingering. Looking across to where Lorena watched him with a serene smile, he found himself wondering if he was the only one.

"Thank you, Michael. We're all very glad you're here."

Doctor Palmer turned to the rest of the group.

"Who would like to start us off today?" she asked. "Does anybody have anything they would like to share?"

There was a protracted silence around the circle, and she tried again.

"Megan? Would you like to start?"

Gregory looked across to where a girl of nineteen or twenty sat with her knees clutched to her chest, her feet balanced precariously on the garden chair. Her hair was lank and greasy, and he noticed she had bitten her nails to the quick.

She shook her head fiercely.

"It's alright," Naomi said. "Maybe you'll feel up to it next time."

She cast her eye around the circle.

"How about you, Ira?"

Gregory leaned forward to see an elderly man seated a couple of chairs to his left. He was dressed in a three-piece suit despite the heat, and seemed to be holding a conversation with himself.

He looked back towards the doctor and thought he caught a flash of sadness, or perhaps professional frustration. He was about to throw her a lifeline, but he was beaten to it.

"I got somethin' to share," Lorena said, in her soft New Jersey twang.

All eyes turned to her.

"Thank you, Lorena, we'd love to hear it," Naomi said. "Go ahead."

"I've been thinkin' about what you said the last time, about defence mechanisms and transference."

Naomi nodded, clearly delighted that somebody had been listening.

"I got a lot of anger inside," she said, and started to twist her hands on her lap. "I thought that's where the demon came from, y'know? I thought it was because of that. Like, I was imagining…somebody else."

She began to rub her arms in a back-and-forth motion, to soothe herself.

"Just lately, I started to wonder whether maybe the demon wasn't anybody else."

"You're sayin' it was real?" Harry demanded, in a sudden surge of unexpected anger. "They're never real—"

Doctor Palmer remained patient, and simply gave him a long look.

"Harry, I'd like you to try that technique we've spoken about before," she said, in a calm voice. "I'd like you to breathe in through your nose and out through your mouth, at a nice steady pace. That's right, well done. Now, what I want you to work on is not rushing towards anger, but to try to listen first. Can you do that for me? Shall we try to listen to what Lorena would like to tell us?"

Gregory watched the man grapple with himself, his face turning blotchy and red with the effort, but suddenly the fight drained from him and he gave a nod.

"Thank you," Doctor Palmer said, and turned back to Lorena. "You were telling us that the demon may not have been who you thought it was."

Lorena nodded. "I—I guess I was wondering if the demon I saw might have been...maybe it was me."

"Why would you think the demon was you, Lorena?"

The woman's lip began to wobble, and she looked up at the doctor with a sadness that was fathoms deep.

"I did something terrible," she whispered. "Unforgivable."

"Nothing is unforgivable," Doctor Palmer said.

Lorena wanted to believe it.

She had to believe it, or it would all have been for nothing.

Around twenty minutes later, the session ended.

Lorena refused to be drawn out any further, and Rosie insisted she was running late to meet the Duke, which led to another angry outburst from Harry—who'd obviously heard one too many tales about the dashing Duke of Warwickshire—and it was clear that no amount of sugary treats or sunshine would be enough to lift his mood.

While Tilda went to help clear up the trays and Doctor Palmer spoke to Harry, Gregory moved like lightning. He began stacking up some of the folding chairs, a couple of which he hooked under his arm, until he reached the chair Doctor Palmer had recently vacated.

"That's kind of you to help," she said, walking back over to retrieve her jacket.

"No trouble," he murmured, and held the jacket open for her, in a gentlemanly fashion.

"Thank you," she said, looking slightly embarrassed. "I'll see you later, Michael. Don't forget, we have a session after lunch."

He nodded, and watched her walk back across the grass, feeling like all kinds of black-hearted villain.

CHAPTER 18

Gregory knew he had only a limited amount of time before the alarm was raised, and so he moved quickly. Having deposited the chairs back in the summer house across the lawn, he jogged back to join the others as they filed into the hospital building and made their way towards the dining room. He saw Doctor Palmer and Tilda amongst them, and deliberately hung back until they were out of sight. Then, he turned and moved swiftly down the corridor towards Doctor Palmer's office, careful to avoid being seen.

Gregory let himself into the office using her master key and shut the door behind him, before moving swiftly to her desk. The previous day, he'd seen Palmer retrieve another key from a mother-of-pearl trinket box she kept on a bookshelf, which he now used to unlock the filing cabinet drawer in her desk.

Working quickly, he rifled through the files, looking for two names in particular.

Lorena Romano and Daniel Barone.

Agonising seconds passed before he found the files, but, when he did, Gregory read the summary notes and then carefully slipped them both back inside the drawer. He replaced the key in its box, then moved swiftly back to the door.

He grasped the door handle and was about to exit when he heard footsteps approaching on the other side.

He snatched his hand away, looking around him in panic. He saw the door handle twist, but the automatic lock prevented it from opening. He heard a sharp intake of breath followed by the sound of fast retreating footsteps as Doctor Palmer realised she was missing a key, and went off to raise the alarm.

Thinking fast now, Gregory's eye fell on one of the large ground floor windows of her office which led directly onto the lawn outside. Unlike the upper levels of the hospital, there were no bars, for there was only a few feet between them and the ground below. They were alarmed, but Tilda had told him the alarm was set every night at nine o'clock, after which time every resident should be inside.

Until then, he was free to open the sash window and make a run for it.

Gregory hiked up the window, which stuck a little at the sides, and after a check to make sure nobody was visible, slid his body through the gap. It was a highly risky manoeuvre, but then, as somebody once said, all of life was risk.

Agile as a cat, he stuck to the edge of the wall until he came within sight of the back door, whereupon he slowed his pace to a casual stroll and wiped his face with the back of his sleeve. He paused, seeming to look at something on the ground, then bent down as if to pick it up, in case anybody should be watching.

When he stepped inside the main building, he saw Doctor Palmer speaking in hushed tones to one of the other nurses, both of whom looked worried.

"Dr Palmer? I found this on the lawn outside. Is it yours?"

He dropped the key card into her open hand.

She looked down at the card and then up at him.

"Thank you for your honesty, Michael," she said quietly. "Not everyone would have done the same thing."

Her words twisted like a knife, but he managed a self-deprecating smile.

"Happy to help," he said.

She turned to the nurse.

"Phil, would you please let the others know the card has been recovered?"

Naomi was still unsure how the card could have fallen from her pocket, but these things happened, and she'd have to be much more vigilant, next time.

"Tilda was telling me you were hoping to join Lorena in the kitchen," she said, as the nurse hurried off to update their colleagues. "You understand, it would be under supervision, but I am happy to allow it if she doesn't mind."

"Thank you," he said. "I'm hoping she'll teach me her recipe for cannoli."

That brought an unexpected smile from the doctor.

"Good luck," she said, laughing. "Apparently, it's a secret family recipe."

There was an awkward pause while they looked at one another, and then Gregory smiled politely and made his way back to his room for a few minutes' respite before lunch. It had been said many times within psychiatric circles that malingering was difficult to sustain twenty-four hours a day but, as he was discovering, feigning illness wasn't so hard when it was only a shade away from the truth.

The hardest thing was having a conscience about it.

Once he was alone again with the door firmly shut, Gregory sank down onto the edge of his bed and let out the pent-up breath he'd been holding. Adrenaline pumped through his body and made him jumpy, but he was hoping he could pass that off as another side-effect of long-term stress.

Either that, or sexual frustration.

He thought about the hour he was due to spend in Naomi Palmer's company later that afternoon and wondered why the hell he liked to make life more complicated for himself; why was he drawn to those who were just as complex and unattainable as himself?

Because Naomi Palmer was troubled. He read it in her eyes—and Gregory, the clinician, wanted to find out why, and try to fix it.

Gregory, the man, wanted the same—only more so.

———

Downstairs, Naomi let herself back into her office with a sigh of relief, and her spirits lifted.

When she'd first read the file on Michael Jones, she'd formed an image of a pampered man-child, one who'd never held down a proper job. She knew it was wrong to make value judgments without knowing the full circumstances, but a psychiatrist was not a robot, and she was as human as the next person. Perhaps, on some deep level, she'd labelled him as the stereotypical wastrel, unequipped to cope with the demands of modern life.

But he'd surprised her.

Michael Jones didn't fit the mould of the pampered rich man, who'd never had to do a hard day's work in his life. Indeed, he barely spoke of his life, nor sought to impress her with his wealth or status, as so many had done before him, as a means to deflect from their other inadequacies. He was quiet and well-spoken, scrupulously polite, and unafraid to pitch in and help when it was needed.

That wasn't to say Michael was entirely free of his demons; they may not have looked like Lorena's, but they were there, nonetheless, and she would uncover them before their time was through. Physically, he was exhausted—that much was plain for all to see—and mentally, he seemed on edge. She wondered if he was suffering from bouts of paranoia, and made a mental note to ask him about it during their next session.

Absently, she moved across the room to close the window, and her hands froze on the ledge.

She was certain she'd closed it, before leaving the room earlier that day.

Hadn't she?

If she'd forgotten, that was the second security breach she'd made that day, which was more than she'd made in the entire two years she'd been employed there.

Unless…

Naomi sank down onto the edge of her sofa to think, unconsciously mirroring Gregory's stance in the room above.

CHAPTER 19

Hospital rules disallowed the use of any sharp implements such as knives, but nobody had banned the use of a rolling pin. So it was that Gregory found himself standing side by side with Lorena Romano, rolling out fresh pastry for the lunchtime crowd.

"You need a little more sugar on there," she told him, and sprinkled a dusting over his rolling pin. Now, try to get the pastry this thin."

She held up a thumb and forefinger to indicate a width of half a centimetre.

Gregory did as he was told and rolled out a large section of sweet pastry dough, which they planned to turn into strawberry tarts. Behind them, Tilda and another nurse by the name of Fletcher sat on high stools, ostensibly supervising Lorena and her new sous chef, whilst in fact talking over the latest celebrity gossip according to the *Hollywood Reporter*. In the background, a radio played 'smooth classics from the seventies', and provided some welcome cover for the conversation Gregory hoped to have.

He glanced over his shoulder, and judged it a good time to start.

Up close, Lorena had a pronounced air of fragility, but her hands were strong and steady as she whipped up the cream that would go inside their tarts. She was dressed simply in jeans and a linen shirt, which billowed at the arms and did little to disguise how painfully thin she had become.

"Where did you learn to cook like this?" he asked. "Did you go to cookery school?"

Lorena looked up in surprise.

"My Nonna taught me," she murmured. "She taught all of us kids, when we were growing up."

"Your nonna? Is that Italian?"

She nodded, and showed him how to cut out the shapes for their tarts. He had a quiet way about him which reminded her of her son, Luca, and she was suddenly transported back to a time when he was four or five, and they'd made cookies together in the kitchen.

Paolo hadn't allowed it, after the boy's sixth birthday.

She felt a sharp pain in her chest, which she recognised immediately as guilt, and raised a hand to rub it away.

Gregory noticed it, but said nothing.

"How did you end up in here?" he asked.

Lorena wondered how much to say.

"I was seeing things," she said eventually. "Things that weren't real."

"You mean, like the demon?"

She nodded.

"What did it look like?"

Lorena glanced at him and then back at the bowl of whipped cream she held in the crook of her arm.

"What d'you mean? It—it was just a demon. He had horns and claws, like an animal."

"Sounds pretty scary," Gregory said. "What colour was it?"

"Colour?"

"It was just black," she said.

Gregory continued to cut out his shapes, setting them in a neat stack for her to fit into the tart dishes.

"Do you still see the demon now?" he asked.

"No," she said, with a smile. "Doctor Palmer says I'm in remission. I just need to spend some more time working out why I saw it in the first place."

Gregory wondered how far to push; it was only the first conversation, after all.

He waited while she took the baking trays filled with individual tarts and put them in the oven for a few minutes.

"Why are you here?" she asked him.

"To find some answers," he replied.

Lorena asked nothing more of him, but handed him the bowl of cream.

"After you've filled the tarts, you can lick the bowl."

"I've heard it's medicinal," he said.

"It doesn't solve all of life's ailments, but it's a good start."

It was raining in Washington DC, but Bill Douglas hardly noticed it pattering against the window.

He was seated inside his friend's home office, making use of the computer while his host gave a lecture to a group of freshmen students over at Georgetown University. It was a charming, artsy neighbourhood west of Capitol Hill, where the cobblestone streets were lined with federal-style architecture and people looking to soak up some culture. Douglas had hoped to take a walk along the Chesapeake and Ohio Canal which intersected with the Potomac River, but thoughts of how Gregory was faring had consumed his mind, particularly since he'd missed his friend's phone call, the previous evening.

He didn't plan to make the same mistake twice, and had kept his mobile phone about him throughout the day, on the off-chance Gregory should call.

After several hours in front of the screen, Douglas decided to call it a day, and made his way back through the faculty building and outside. It was still raining, fat, warm droplets which plastered his hair to the crown of his head, and he hurried towards the road, on the other side of which he'd parked the rental car he and Gregory had picked up in Baltimore a week before.

The streets were unusually empty, most people having made their way indoors to avoid the shower, so there was nobody to witness the dark SUV crawl slowly from its parking space. Nor did they see the man with his briefcase raised over his head, who took a quick glance in either direction before stepping out into the street.

Douglas heard the car before he saw it.

A sharp roar, as the engine accelerated, followed by a squeal of tyres. He turned, but there was no time to run or throw himself back.

In the seconds that followed, he saw his whole life reflected in the car's tinted windshield, a million tiny fragments of memory that made up the whole person.

And then, darkness.

CHAPTER 20

Four o'clock could not come soon enough.

Gregory was counting the hours until he could put a call through to Hawk and Douglas but, before then, he had an emotional gauntlet to run, and it came in the form of Dr Naomi Palmer.

Having apparently decided he was not about to bolt from the stable, Tilda allowed him to find his own way along to her office, which he did for the second time that day. His hands were clammy as he reached up to knock on her door—a sign he took clearly to mean he shouldn't consider a serious career in cat burglary any time soon, if the merest bit of pocket-pinching was enough to have him sweating like a Sunday roast.

The door swung open, and she offered him a polite smile.

"Hello again, Michael. Come in."

It was like returning to the scene of the crime, he thought.

"You look pale," she said. "Are you feeling alright?"

He pasted a smile on his face. "Yes, thank you."

She gestured him towards the seating area, and he took the same seat he had the previous day, with his back facing the wall.

"It's funny, what you can tell about a person from the places they choose to sit," she said. "For example, it's interesting that you always choose the least vulnerable seat, which allows you to protect your back and see the rest of the room clearly—for some people, that can be an indicator that they have trust issues."

That was true, he thought. He'd never been comfortable sitting with his back to an open room, just as he preferred to be near the door, which would allow him to make a speedy departure should the need arise.

He hadn't realised he was so easy to read, but perhaps it depended on the reader.

"Would you like some water?"

"No, thank you."

He would've preferred coffee, but that didn't seem to be on offer today.

In fact, he'd noticed a distinct coolness to her manner which was at odds with her warm expression of thanks earlier in the day. His rational mind told him there could be many reasons for that; he was not her only patient, and who knew what manner of crises she had overseen that day, which might account for her own lowered mood?

Instinct, on the other hand...

Instinct told him, in no uncertain terms, that she *knew*.

His eyes strayed over to the sash window, which was now firmly closed.

"Are you feeling the heat?" she asked, sweetly. "You could always open a window."

Gregory looked at her with unconcealed admiration. "I'm perfectly comfortable, thank you," he said.

She clicked the end of her pen with slightly more force than was necessary, and crossed her legs.

"Is there anything in particular you'd like to talk about, Michael?"

"Not really," he said.

She gritted her teeth. "Tilda tells me you suffered a night terror, last night," she said, and something of the warmth crept back into her voice.

She was a woman who couldn't help but care, Gregory thought, with another sharp stab of guilt. Even through her anger, she wanted to know how to help him.

"Do you remember what happened in the dream?"

Of course, he remembered.

He remembered all of them.

"Not really." He shrugged.

She sighed, and tapped the edge of her pen against her notepad while she thought of a way to draw him out.

"Tell me about your family, Michael."

"What do want to know?"

"Anything you'd like to tell me."

He was about to say something trite, but instead found himself doing something entirely unexpected.

He began to talk.

"My mother and father divorced when I was four," he said, grudgingly. "My father remarried. My mother..."

He stopped, wondering how much Michael Jones should say, without treading on Alexander Gregory's toes.

"Your mother—?"

"She didn't cope very well with that," he said.

"That must have been difficult for you," she said. "What kind of relationship do you have with your father?"

"The non-existent kind," he said.

"I'm so—"

"Don't be," he interjected. "It's no loss to me."

She wasn't so sure. "Describe your father to me, Michael."

"I wouldn't know how. I haven't seen him in a very long time."

"Describe what you remember of him, then."

He looked into her patient eyes, and then around the room, afraid to delve into the box of memories he kept securely locked in his mind.

"He—" His voice broke, and he tried again. "He's a financier—or, at least, he was. He's retired now."

She waited, having learned the value of silence.

"Money was important to him but people...rather less so. He was very authoritarian, and didn't appreciate outward expressions of emotion."

"How did that make you feel, Michael?"

Repressed. Frightened. Angry. Abandoned.

"Grateful," he said, coldly. "Through his own actions, he taught me to understand the difference between 'right' and 'wrong.'"

He was a melting pot of emotion, she thought, just ready to bubble over. But these things were best done in stages.

"What about your mother?" she asked. "You don't mention her very often."

Or at all, she amended.

That was another curious discrepancy, when she compared the man seated in front of her with the other patients she'd known. Few, if any, failed to mention the relationship they had with their mother because—for better or for worse—it was a defining feature of their personal journey.

She watched him, and wondered what lay behind those luminous green eyes.

"There's very little to say, other than what I've already told you."

"I don't believe that," she said. "Why don't you start by describing her to me?"

Tell her, Michael. Tell her what I'm like.

He closed her eyes, trying to block out the memory of her voice, the way she'd smelled, or the feel of her skin.

"She wasn't a very good mother," he said simply. "She abused us all, never showed a scrap of remorse, and then she died last year."

There, he thought. *Have at it.*

Something in his eyes warned her that that was enough for one day, and she set her notepad down.

"Some women bear children but are incapable of mothering them, afterwards," she said. "Perhaps, your mother had her own struggles."

He almost laughed, but the sound would have held no mirth.

"So, I should feel sorry for her?"

Here it was, she thought. The anger he kept so well contained.

"You don't need to feel sorry for her," Palmer said. "You only need to understand one thing."

He cocked his head.

"It wasn't your fault they abandoned you, Michael. Your mother and father are their own people, and their decisions reflect their own mental state at the time, not the people whose lives they impacted."

He knew that, Gregory thought. He'd read all around the subject, had been to his own share of therapy sessions and told himself something similar, most days.

Why, then, did it sound so different, coming from this woman's lips?

Palmer weighed up the consequences of telling him a small piece of personal information about herself, against the positive value it might have in making him feel less alone.

For he was surely the loneliest person she'd ever known.

"You aren't the only one to have ever felt abandoned," she said quietly. "My parents abandoned me at birth, in a basket outside a hospital."

Gregory listened and, for a moment, it was as though the tables were turned again.

"Have you been able to forgive?"

"I hated these people I'd never known," she admitted. "For the longest time. But then, I realised something important. I was focusing too much on their negative action, and not on the many positive things that came from it, such as the loving adoptive parents I grew up with, or the opportunities I've had in life. I don't know what led them to leave me out there, that day, but whatever the reason, it can't have been good. Perhaps they did the right thing."

Gregory understood why she'd breached a practice guideline, and was grateful for it.

"Your parents abandoned you, while my mother kept me, but there was no 'right' outcome," he said. "It was out of our hands, from the start."

She nodded.

"So I guess what you're trying to tell me is—I need to get over myself and stop blaming my mother?"

"Well, you said it."

They both grinned like fools, then he looked up at the clock on the wall.

"Time's up," he said softly.

But as he headed for the door, she had one last word for him.

"Michael?"

He turned, and waited.

"Please, the next time you'd like to see the notes I'm keeping of our sessions, just ask me. There's no need to steal my key card."

He inclined his head, and thought it was a blessing she had no idea whose file he'd really been interested in.

CHAPTER 21

As the clock struck four, Gregory dialled his friend's number and waited patiently while it rang.

Across the room, he saw that Tilda was engrossed in the same magazine she'd read cover to cover the day before.

The number went to voicemail.

Gregory told himself to remain calm, and checked the number against the one Douglas had given him, before re-dialling.

No answer.

He stared at the receiver, and tried Hawk's number instead.

This time, the phone was answered almost immediately.

"Hey, cuz."

There was a temptation to download all the information he had learned over the past day or so, but he knew the score—Hawk would ask the questions, and he would answer. That would reduce the chances of a slip-up, on his part.

"So, how're you feeling?"

Gregory knew it was a polite opener, not a genuine enquiry.

"Pretty good today, thanks."

"Oh yeah? That's great, really great," Hawk said, injecting the necessary enthusiasm into his voice, to be expected of a close relative. "Did you make any new friends?"

"Yeah, I did, actually. One of the other residents here, Lorena, is a mean pastry chef. She's letting me tag along in the kitchen."

He heard Hawk's sharp intake of breath at the other end of the line.

"She sounds...nice," he managed, working hard to keep the excitement from his voice.

It wasn't every day you learned that your star witness wasn't wearing a pair of cement shoes, somewhere in the East River.

"Yeah, seems to be," Gregory replied. "She says she sees demons, but I'm not convinced. I reckon it's all the sugar, going to her head."

He winked at Tilda, who looked up from her magazine briefly, before immersing herself again.

"How d'you know they're not real?"

This, too, was important information, if Gregory was suggesting he thought her symptoms were fake.

"She said the demon was all black, with no other colour," he said, under his breath, and left it at that.

Individuals who were simulating illnesses like schizophrenia, or other disorders where hallucinations were commonplace, often said their visions were in black and white. However, studies consistently showed that real visions almost always came in full technicolour.

A small but vital distinction.

"Actually, I met her husband, too," Gregory continued, keeping his tone steady. "I almost ran into the poor guy, just after I'd spoken to you, yesterday."

Hawk was silent for a couple of seconds.

"Small world," he said, lightly.

"Yeah, seemed a friendly guy. Warned me about the ridge outside being dangerous. Nice, how thoughtful some people can be, isn't it?"

"We Yanks are a friendly bunch," Hawk said. "You—ah—meet anyone else?"

"Nice old lady called Kitty Steenberg," he said.

"Kitty Steenberg—the arsonist?"

Gregory felt his stomach shudder, and realised it was shock.

"What's that?"

"Yeah, that's an old one," Hawk said. "The story was everywhere. She's the Vanderkamp heiress who burned their summer mansion to the ground, with her brother, husband and son all still inside. She claimed the voices told her to do it, but it was widely known at the time that Terrence Steenberg was going to leave her for another woman. Her brother had always been close to the husband, and her son looked just like him. She served time, but then the State gave her compassionate parole a couple of years ago, provided she lives the rest of her days in a secure wing, with twenty-four-hour supervision."

He'd been guilty of the very thing he told his junior staff to be careful of, Gregory realised—taking a patient at face value.

"Who else you got locked up in there?" Hawk laughed. "Jack the Ripper?"

Gregory was almost afraid to say, unless it turned out to be true.

"I forgot to mention, I looked up the name of your doctor on the website and"—he let out a long whistle of appreciation—"you lucked out there, cuz."

Gregory thought back to their most recent therapy session.

"You might be right."

There must have been something in his voice, for Hawk spoke seriously again.

"I'm only supposed to visit you at the end of the first week, to give you a chance to settle in," he said. "But if you need me to drive up there and see you, I will."

Gregory almost said *yes*, but then he remembered that Hawk had already risked himself once by dropping him off at the facility. It would be dangerous for him to make an unnecessary trip, just to put him at ease.

Besides he wasn't supposed to be staying all that long.

Was he?

"Hey, I tried calling Uncle Bill, earlier," he said lightly. "Have you heard from him?"

"Can't say that I have," Hawk said. "Maybe try him again?"

"Uh-huh…I keep missing him, I guess. He wasn't at home last night, either."

This gave Agent Hawk pause.

"I'll check on him," he said. "Make sure he's eating right, and all that stuff."

"Tell him to turn his phone on," Gregory muttered.

"Right. Stay focused, cuz."

Gregory tried Douglas's number a couple more times, but kept receiving an automated voicemail message. The fact that he hadn't been able to reach his friend for the second day running was a source of alarm—Bill Douglas might give the impression of a bookish academic, but he was one of the most reliable people he'd ever known, never having been late for a single appointment in the decade he'd known him. It was highly unlikely he would have missed his—by now—numerous phone calls, unless there was good reason.

Given the present situation, all manner of worst-case scenarios began to play out in his mind.

"Everything alright, honey? You seem a little upset."

He'd forgotten Tilda was still there.

"Just—missing the outside world," he said.

Tilda set down her magazine and let out a small sound of sympathy.

"Ah now, don't you fret," she said. "Everybody feels the same, in their first week. But, after you've been here a couple of months, it'll seem like home."

Gregory stopped dead.

"I won't be here that long," he said, with a confidence he didn't altogether feel. "I'm already feeling much better than I was."

Tilda smiled one of her big, empty smiles.

"Of course, you are."

"Say that again?"

Tony "The Fist" Garcia had spent the past hour trying to think of the best way of telling his boss the news he'd just received, but there was no way to sugar-coat an ugly truth.

And, boy, this one was ugly as they came.

"That kid you asked me to look into, the one from the hospital? He's not who he says he is."

He knew it, Paolo thought. First time he'd set his eyes on that arrogant little jabroni, he'd known somethin' was off.

"Who the hell is he then?"

"Some guy called Gregory—Doctor Alexander Gregory. Passing himself off as Michael Jones. Took a bit longer than usual, had to grease a few more wheels, but we got it in the end."

"He must've had help," Paolo said.

Tony nodded. "You bet your ass he did, boss. He's got a trail sayin' he's Michael Jones, this rich kid. Turns out, it's only half the story. The guy changed his name from Michael to Alexander back in the day, and made a new life for himself." Tony shrugged. "So, I tell one o' the guys to Google him, right? And he pops up at some hospital in England."

"Yeah, he sounded like one of them," Paolo snarled.

"So, what do I do?" Tony said, and threw his arms wide to punctuate his moment of triumph. "I ring the number and ask to speak to him. Y'know what they tell me, boss? That he's away at some kinda symposium or some shit like that. You never gonna guess where—"

"Where?" Paolo growled, in no mood for guessing games.

"Quantico!"

"Son of a bitch," Paolo breathed. "So—what? The Feds send 'im in to find some dirt on Danny? That it?"

"I don't think that's it, boss," Tony said, turning an uncomfortable shade of puce that was only partly to do with hypertension.

"Then…" Paolo trailed off, as the unbelievable truth hit him like a sledgehammer.

He held his head in his hands for a moment, then looked up at his second-in-command with eyes that were black with rage.

"You gotta be kidding me."

Tony held up his hands.

"Boss, I wish I were. Believe me."

"Lorena would never do this," he said. "The bitch hates me, but she's not stupid."

Wisely, Tony remained silent.

"You better not be lying to me," Paolo said, and the tone was ice cold.

Tony shook his head.

"Never, boss. Whaddya wanna do about it?"

Paolo could barely think past the haze of anger, which fell like a red mist. If Lorena had been in the room he knew he would have killed her, right there and then.

"We got a good lawyer," Tony said. "He'd rip her apart, if she ever made it to court. After bein' at the Buchanan all this time, her credibility is zero, 'specially once we tell 'em she's been seein' the demons, right?"

Paolo was only half listening. It was true that wives couldn't rat on their husbands, but there were ways around it. He hadn't always been as careful as he should've been around Lorena...especially after thirty years. After that, a man should be able to trust his goddamn wife.

The Feds had found a way to get to her, alright.

"Get me the hospital file again," he said, in a voice completely devoid of emotion. "I got an idea."

CHAPTER 22

At dinner, Gregory found himself seated between a rock and a hard place—otherwise, known as Harry and Marco. Tilda had taken a seat on another table beside Lorena and Megan, and was encouraging her to eat, while Kitty held court on a table with Ira and a couple of others. Spotting him, she waved a heavily-bejewelled hand in his direction, and blew him a kiss.

He could only be glad the dinner wasn't candlelit, following Hawk's earlier revelation.

"So, kid. How you settlin' in?"

Harry took an enormous bite of his cheeseburger, and didn't quite manage to catch the ketchup before it oozed from either side of his mouth to join the cemetery of crumbs in his beard.

"See you got the nice doctor," Marco put in. "Doctor Hot-Stuff."

Gregory took a bite of his own cheeseburger, then wished he hadn't. Worry about his friend was churning around his belly, and a cheeseburger—even one of the gourmet ones they served up at the Buchanan—did little to help.

"We both got lumbered with Kaufmann," Harry said, jerking a greasy thumb between himself and Marco.

"You don't like him?"

Harry leaned forward and spoke in an undertone.

"He's in their *pockets*."

Gregory's ears pricked.

"Whose pockets?"

"Who the hell d'you think? The government. The insurance companies. Both of 'em. All of them! That's why they got poor schmucks like me droolin' down my chin all night, so they can cash those nice, big cheques."

"You don't think the medication helps you?"

Harry's fingers curled around the burger, sending fat dollops of ketchup and mustard slopping onto his plate.

"You think I need help?" he asked, belligerently.

Gregory was unfazed.

"Don't we all?"

Harry blinked, and then let out a roaring hoot of laughter which drew several eyes from around the room.

"You're alright, kid."

Gregory took that as high praise, and risked another question.

"What else d'you think is going on around here?"

"How long you got?" Marco asked, with a snigger. "They had to get rid of ol' Kellerman. Heard he was helpin' himself to the medicine cabinet."

"Don't forget what happened to Danny," Harry muttered. "Cover-up, if ever I saw."

"Danny?"

"Yeah, Danny. *The Baron*," Marco said. "You never heard of him?"

"He's a Brit," Harry said. "He don't know shit."

The two men laughed and, although it might have been at his expense, Gregory didn't mind. It was true, after all, that he hadn't known much about the Mafia until about a week ago.

"Danny Barone was a made man," Marco explained. "Part of the Romano family."

Gregory tried to look surprised, and looked towards the table where Lorena was seated.

"Romano? You mean—?"

"Yeah, Lorena's husband," Harry said, in an undertone. "Why d'you think Kaufmann's walkin' around in a brand-new suit? The guy comes up here to visit her, every week, and leaves a nice fat wad by the front desk."

Gregory filed that away for later.

"What happened to Danny?"

"Barone was up here for amnesia, or some crap like that. Said he couldn't remember. A couple of weeks later, he was gone," Marco said.

"Gone?"

"That's what he said," Harry replied, taking a long swill of coke. "The decorators were out there paintin' the windows, and the stupid sonofabitch stole himself a bottle of turpentine. Drank damn near three-quarters, before they found him."

"Yeah, and Kaufmann was his doctor," Marco said. "He said it was suicide, but who's to know any different? Poor bastard."

"Lorena better watch herself," Harry said. "Romano wanted rid of Danny and jus' look what happened."

"Surely, the hospital wouldn't allow—"

"You know nothin' kid," Harry said, not unkindly. "You got that look in your eye, like you're still fightin'. Me and Marco? We know when to stop bangin' our heads against that big stone wall. You gotta wake up and smell the roses, cos they stink."

Before Gregory could formulate a response, they were interrupted by Doctor Kaufmann himself, whose ears must have been burning. He entered the dining room with a man of around thirty in tow, blond and blue-eyed, who bore a passing resemblance to a young Robert Redford.

"Good evening, everyone!"

Kaufmann clapped his hands together.

"I'd like to introduce you all to a new resident," he said. "This is Noah. I hope you'll make him feel welcome."

Kaufmann glanced around the room, then fixed his eye on their table of three, and the chair that stood empty beside them. Gregory sighed inwardly, feeling incapable of making further conversation when, all the while, his mind wandered in circles around a single question.

Where was Bill Douglas?

Harry and Marco looked equally sullen; having only recently come around to accepting Gregory into their small world, they were in no mood to extend their sunny personalities beyond that which was already established.

"Hello, gentlemen," Kaufmann said, flashing one of his megawatt smiles. "Michael? As you've only recently joined us, perhaps you could take Mr Wilson under your wing and help him to feel at home?"

Gregory could think of nothing more inconvenient.

"Of course," he muttered, and gave Noah the 'once-over'.

Eyes over-bright. Septum eroded. Nails picked away to the quick. Mouth gurning.

Addict.

"Lay off the dust, kid," Harry told the new arrival, taking the words out of Gregory's mouth. "You don't wanna spoil that pretty face."

Gregory took the executive decision to deposit Noah into the capable hands of Tilda, who proceeded to cluck over him like a mother hen, as he'd known she would. He took the chance to head back to the telephone room, intending to try Douglas's number one more time.

But the room was occupied.

I need to speak to Bill Douglas.

Where's Bill?

He was about to bang on the door and demand they clear out, that it was an emergency, but the panic attack caught him unawares, robbing him of breath. The pressure of it crushed his chest like a vice, so that his breath came in short, hissing gulps. He leaned back against the wall in the corridor and tried to slow down, remembering the techniques he'd been shown, and had shown others.

He began to shake and sweat, his eyes swimming with dark spots, and he slid to the floor.

"Michael!"

Through the fog, he saw a pair of feet running towards him, clad in plain black pumps.

A moment later, he smelled her scent.

"Naomi," he slurred.

"What did you take, Michael?" she asked, urgently.

He shook his head, one hand rubbing at his chest as if to relieve the pressure.

"Nothing. Panic attack."

"Okay. Look at me," she said firmly.

He dragged his head up, and her face swam before him.

"Breathe in through your nose for two—count with me. One…two….Then, out through your mouth…one…two…"

One of the other nurses hurried over, but Doctor Palmer waved them away.

"His colour's looking better," she said. "I'll take care of him."

Gregory rested his head back against the wall and took a few more deep breaths, before rubbing his sleeve over his face.

"Sorry," he muttered.

"There's nothing to apologise for," she said, and held out a hand to help him come to his feet. "What brought on the attack?"

I'm not who you think I am.

The only people who know who I really am are at the end of a telephone line.

The person closest to me, a surrogate father, has been incommunicado for two days.

The Mafia know I'm here.

You wouldn't believe me, if I told you.

"I was hoping to make a phone call, but all the lines are taken," he said.

She understood how crucial it was for residents to speak with the important people in their lives, and was curious to know who fell into that category for him.

"You can use the telephone in my office—but no more than ten minutes. I'm making an exception, Michael, so please don't abuse it."

He nodded.

"Thank you."

But there was still no answer from Douglas's phone, and he ran an agitated hand over the back of his neck, wondering what else he could do. Hawk had already promised to look into things, but it would be another twenty-four hours before the designated calling time.

He didn't think twice, but dialled Hawk's number.

No answer.

After the fifth attempt, Gregory replaced the receiver carefully back into its cradle.

Be careful you don't go too near the edge, Romano had said.

Perhaps he'd already fallen.

CHAPTER 23

Gregory must have dreamed a thousand dreams, but none quite so real as the one which held his mind captive through the small hours of the morning.

He saw himself walking through a pine-scented wood, along a winding, single-track road. The air around him was heavy with a decay so ripe, he could taste its sweetness on the air. No birds called in the branches or flew overhead; there were no people or cars, or even the comforting scurry of animals beneath the forest canopy.

Dark places, his mother used to say. *Monsters lurk in small spaces, and dark places.*

He turned back, but the view was identical; an inescapable void of road, where the only option was to continue walking.

He saw a light ahead of him now—a distant glow, nothing more—and began to run, his white trainers pounding the earth until his muscles ached and his lungs screamed.

But he didn't stop.

He kept running towards the unknown, beyond the edge of the forest until he reached a tall set of gates.

Don't lose your pass.

You'll be shot on sight without it.

But he had no pass, and no means of entry. The gates were locked and barred, the padlock rusted with age and disuse.

Beyond the gates, he could see a garden, well-tended and fragrant, bathed in sunlight, and a house of beige bricks. Twenty or more people sat in a circle, and in the centre of them all was Bill Douglas.

Come on, Michael!

He tried the lock again, but it held fast.

He tried to call for help, but the words lodged in his throat, unspoken and unheard.

Bill! his mind screamed. *Open the gates, Bill!*

I don't have the key, Michael.

The others turned to look at him, and he recognised them all. Patients he'd helped, women he'd loved, and those he hadn't been able to love, nor to help.

They all watched him now, standing on the other side of the gate.

Slowly, one by one, they stood and raised their hands to point.

Behind you, they chanted. *There's a demon behind you.*

Don't look, Lorena said, stepping out from the woods. *Don't look behind. Only look forward.*

As she stepped out into the road, he saw that her face was grey and mottled, the skin scorched around her mouth, melted away like wax.

In her hand, she held a bottle, which she raised to her lips.

Lupara bianca!

She toasted him, and poured the liquid down her throat.

No! NO!

He shouted a warning, but it was too late.

The others in the circle turned away, the man who had been Michael now forgotten. Their faces became indistinct and their voices too soft to hear, and he rattled the gates, crying out to them, begging them to remember him.

Then, there was nothing but himself and the darkness, which was complete.

Gregory awoke to find his arms and legs restrained, and he struggled wildly.

Demons, his feverish mind whispered.

Monsters in the dark.

"You need to stay calm, Michael."

Tilda's voice sounded different, more detached.

"You were screaming and thrashing in your sleep, waking up the rest of the ward," she said. "We can't have this, every night."

He heard a tear, and realised it was the sound of her opening a fresh syringe packet.

"No," he said. "I don't need—"

"Your sleep habits are disruptive to the other residents and dangerous to yourself," she said, in the same maddening tone.

He squeezed his eyes shut, ordering himself to think.

Think!

"Please, I don't want any medication," he muttered.

But he knew that he'd signed away some of his rights, when he'd entered the Buchanan. He'd been so confident it would never become an issue. He, the Great Psychologist, would be too smart, too savvy to fall foul of the clinician's dispensary.

"I'm calm now," he said.

He hated the sound of his own pleading voice. Didn't it resemble all the others he'd heard at Southmoor? All the times he'd taken the decision to medicate, no matter how correct it was, he'd removed somebody's agency to choose and now he knew what that felt like.

"Please," he said again. "I don't need it."

Tilda stood over him now, and the early dawn light at her back cast her face in shadow. In her hand, she held the syringe.

Slowly, she lowered it again.

"If this happens again, Michael, you'll need to be sedated."

"It won't," he said, and hoped it was true.

CHAPTER 24

Life at the Buchanan was beginning to resemble the Twilight Zone.

After wielding a syringe above his head in the small hours of the morning, Tilda had returned to his room at breakfast-time wearing her usual smile, behaving as if nothing had happened, and had even asked if he'd slept well. Choosing to ignore the question, Gregory had attempted to use the telephone room but, without being able to explain why the matter was so urgent, he'd been given the same rebuttal as any of the other patients and no amount of arguing or cajolery had worked to change her mind on the subject.

There had been no sign of Lorena at breakfast, which had given Gregory further cause for concern, in addition to his existing anxiety around Bill Douglas's whereabouts—and Agent Hawk's, come to that. As far as he could tell, there were a limited number of explanations as to what had happened.

The first, and by far the most preferable to him, was that Douglas had simply given him the wrong number to call. That would explain why he'd been unable to get through, but was unlikely—the idea that Bill would have written down the wrong digits without checking seemed flagrantly ridiculous.

Besides, even when he'd tried the number the FBI had provided to Douglas, that had also come to nothing, which undermined the whole premise.

Which brought him to the second possible explanation.

It was possible that Douglas had, through some mismanagement of time or forgetfulness, not been around to take Gregory's calls. This was a less appealing option, but still preferable to the third, which was, by far, his least favourite.

The third explanation was, of course, that some dreadful incident had prevented his friend from answering Gregory's calls; something serious enough to prevent him answering for the past two days. With the added worry of Agent Hawk not having answered the telephone last night, Gregory thought it was a strong possibility the Family had found out about Lorena's duplicity and were in the process of putting a stop to it.

Which meant, Gregory thought, that Lorena was in more danger than ever before.

"—Michael?"

He blinked, and realised suddenly that he'd been asked a question, which awaited an answer. Twenty pairs of eyes had turned to where he was seated, directly opposite Doctor Palmer, in that morning's group therapy session.

"I'm sorry, could you repeat the question?"

Distracted, he could almost hear the nurses say. *Spending more time in his internal world, rather than in reality.*

"Of course," Doctor Palmer said. "I asked you if there's anything you'd like to share with the group?"

They were seated in the library, this time, where the central tables had been pushed back to allow folding chairs to be set up in a circle. He couldn't decide which was more peaceful—the rustle of the trees and the breeze coming off the mountain, or the musty smell of old books and the sight of dust motes dancing in the sunlight, which streamed through the windows. Either way, it was preferable to the larger therapy rooms at Southmoor, with their dank smell and uninspiring view of the concrete quadrangle outside.

He looked around the circle of residents, whose number had now swelled to twenty-four, including Noah, and wondered how many of them gained something from Doctor Palmer's psychotherapeutic methods as much as the opportunity to be *seen* and *heard*. In the sessions with his patients back home, he spent much of his time trying to make them feel comfortable enough to talk, but it was often the case that he needed just one person to start the ball rolling.

"I had a bad dream last night," he said quietly. "I'd like to talk about that."

"Please, go ahead."

He proceeded to set out what happened in his dream, omitting the part Lorena and Bill Douglas had played in it, for obvious reasons. There was something comforting in recounting the details to a roomful of people—there was less to fear, when he was not alone.

"It's interesting you found the gates barred to you," Doctor Palmer said. "Why do you think that was, Michael?"

He was about to launch into a full and complete analysis drawn from his academic research around the Freudian meaning of dreams, but stopped himself just in time. Still, the average dreamer could exercise common sense, so he applied that, instead.

"I think the locked gate represents my constant feeling that I don't belong, which probably relates to the feelings of abandonment I have in respect of my mother."

Lorena, he noticed, was giving him her undivided attention.

"In that case, what do you think it meant when your friend on the other side of the gates told you they didn't have the key?"

Gregory gave her a lopsided smile.

"I think it meant that somewhere, deep in my own psyche, I know there's only one person with the key—and that's me."

Dr Palmer smiled.

"One more question," she said. "What is the gate?"

There was a short silence while he considered the question—*really* considered it.

"The gate is my mind," he said. "It's every defence mechanism I've ever built to keep out the rest of the world."

Just like the stone wall in his previous dream, Gregory added silently.

"It isn't so much that anybody's locked *me out*," he said. "It's more that I locked *myself in*."

"Well done," Palmer said softly.

Gregory felt no sense of shame or unease, as he might have expected to, and instead experienced a sudden outpouring of gratitude to the assorted personalities sitting around him, who listened quietly even as they struggled with their own problems.

"Well, shit," Harry said, bursting the bubble. "My dreams are all X-rated, Doc, and, let me tell you, I ain't put up any defences to speak of."

He gave a bawdy laugh, which set the rest of the group off.

"*Thank you* for sharing that, Harry," Doctor Palmer said, with the air of one who'd heard it before. "Does anybody else have anything they'd like to share?"

"Michael said he felt abandoned by his mother," Lorena said, and heads swivelled in her direction. "Does it always mess people up, Doctor Palmer? Maybe…are there any who might not feel that way?"

Though the question was directed to her, Doctor Palmer looked towards the man she knew as Michael, and invited him to answer.

He smiled, understanding it was a test to see whether he had internalised anything of their discussion the previous day.

"Doctor Palmer and I were talking about this yesterday," he said to Lorena. "The fact is, I've spent a long time feeling angry with my mother and father, wishing they'd been different. I've spent a long time looking outward, wondering how other families were. But maybe my parents couldn't be anything other than what they were. Perhaps, I've been holding on to this anger as an excuse not to get on with my life and really live it."

He paused, swallowing the hard truth of it, and finding it a very bitter pill.

"I don't think everybody feels that way, but, even if they do, it shouldn't last forever."

Palmer had been watching Lorena's face, and wondered if this was the moment to press her about the disclosure she'd made during their previous group session, when she said she had done something unforgivable.

"Why do you ask about abandonment, Lorena? Is there anything you'd like to share?"

Lorena looked around the other faces in the group, all of them strangers, really, but found no judgment.

"I—my family were…" She hardly knew how to describe growing up in the world she had, so didn't even try. "They had certain values, and very particular ideas about what girls should and shouldn't do. I was raised strict Catholic, which meant no sex before marriage. Period."

"That's one reason I'm glad to be Jewish," Harry joked, with another of his full-bodied laughs.

Even Lorena managed a smile, albeit one tinged with sadness.

"When I was fifteen, I met a boy at church. Ironic, right? They sent me to church so I'd learn how to be good," she said, with a short laugh. "This boy used to walk me to the corner, where I'd get the bus home. He was a nice boy," she whispered.

"What was his name?" Doctor Palmer asked.

Lorena raised eyes that were suddenly full of tears.

"Luca," she said. She had named her youngest son after him.

"What happened, Lorena?"

"We did what young people do," she said, with a wistful smile. "But I was too young, and when my father found out, he—"

"What? He report him to the cops?"

"No," Lorena said, and wondered what it must be like to think of the police as friends, or guardians. The truth was, she'd never found out what her father had done to Luca Brattoli, but imagining was bad enough.

"It doesn't matter now," she said, raggedly. "What matters is that I found out I was having a baby. The night I told my dad, he nearly killed me."

It seemed so small a word to describe the injuries he'd inflicted; some she kept as scars on her body, others which ran much deeper than that.

There was, unusually, total silence around the room, with none of the usual fidgeting or rustling or skin-picking that usually characterised these group sessions.

"My dad wanted to throw me out," she said. "Mom managed to persuade him to let me stay—but only if I got rid of the baby."

"Abortion?" Doctor Palmer asked, carefully.

Lorena shook her head. "Abortion was classified as a mortal sin, and besides, I couldn't do it—"

She took a minute to compose herself before continuing.

"They sent me to live with my Nonna. I thought, maybe, as the baby grew, things might get better. Dad might change his mind…It didn't work out that way."

She reached across the table for the box of tissues Doctor Palmer had already laid out, and dabbed her tears.

"I had the baby there, with Nonna as midwife," she said. "I'd never known a feeling like it…the love was…"

She stopped herself, dragging another tissue from the box to scrub at her eyes. It had the unfortunate effect of smearing the mascara she'd been allowed to apply earlier that day, which only seemed to add to her present vulnerability.

"My father came around the next day," she said, in a curious, flat voice. "I was sleeping when he took the baby away."

There was a special sympathy reserved for children, even amongst the most hardened or insane of criminals, and even Kitty Steenberg gave a horrified gasp.

"What happened to the baby?" Gregory asked.

"I never knew," Lorena said. "I only had the one night with my baby. I could—I know, if I really tried, I could have found out what happened to it."

To her.

"But they told me it was for the best, and I should forget all about it. You have to understand, it's all I knew. All I was ever good for was getting married, and my father told me nobody would want me, if they knew I was…that I was damaged goods."

"That must have been very hurtful to hear," Doctor Palmer said, and Gregory could see she was trying hard to bank down her anger on the subject.

Lorena nodded.

"I've tortured myself all these years, wondering… just wondering what happened and whether my baby was still"—her voice broke—"whether it was even alive. Every year, I baked a cake and said a prayer."

"That's a lovely thought," Doctor Palmer said.

"D'you think so?" Lorena said, a bit desperately. "D'you think, if they knew what happened…if they knew, they'd forgive me?"

Doctor Palmer smiled.

"Perhaps they'd come to the same conclusion as Michael, which is to understand that the decision you made—which was not to look for your baby after it was taken—was made in difficult circumstances. Really, it had little to do with them and more to do with you, and the

169

life you weren't able to give them. They may feel there's nothing to forgive."

Lorena began to cry softly, but they were not tears of unhappiness. In the Catholic sense, she felt absolved.

Gregory turned his gaze towards Doctor Palmer, whose own life history must surely have made that a difficult conversation. She maintained a calm exterior and moved on to talk to the next patient, so he might never have guessed she was affected by Lorena's tale.

But then, perhaps she hadn't realised exactly what Lorena had tried to tell her.

That she, Naomi Palmer, was the baby Lorena had lost.

CHAPTER 25

Gregory waited for Dr Palmer beside her office door.

He had no intention of telling her what he suspected to be the case regarding her relationship with Lorena Romano—it was mere supposition, at that point. However, whilst Naomi may not have been aware of the arrangement Lorena had previously made with the FBI, he certainly was, and it enabled him to draw the most likely conclusion. There had to be a reason why Lorena came to Buchanan Hospital and, as Bill Douglas had frequently told him, the truth of a matter was never half as complicated as it appeared. That seemed to be the case here, and would explain why she'd been simulating hallucinations. The FBI had been so concerned with knowing why she'd suddenly missed their rendezvous, they'd focused their attention on what seemed the two most plausible reasons: namely, that she was genuinely ill and in need of treatment, or that her husband had packed her off into the wilderness to await an accidental death of some description.

Perhaps Lorena, knowing she was intending to go into the Witness Protection Program, decided at the last moment to see the child she'd managed to track down. The only way to do that was to feign a serious mental break, which would see her sent up to the same place she already knew was a favourite of her husband's.

That might have been the end of it, Gregory thought, if it weren't for one thing.

There was still every chance her husband would find out about her intention to betray him, and try to silence her before she could.

Which was why it was imperative he reached Agent Hawk or Bill Douglas—the only two people in the world who knew the truth.

"Hello, Michael," Doctor Palmer said, as she approached the door. "Is everything all right? We don't have our next one-on-one session until this afternoon."

"I was hoping to use your telephone," he said.

She was relieved to find that was all.

"I'm sorry, Michael. I made an exception last night because you were distressed, but the rest of the time, ordinary rules must apply. They're the same for everyone."

She unlocked her door, expecting him to move off.

Instead, Gregory followed her into the office. He was used to conversing with fellow members of staff in their offices, and thought nothing of it. Unfortunately, he'd forgotten that Doctor Palmer knew him only as 'Michael Jones', and therefore found the action alarming.

"I understand the rules are there for a reason, but this really is an emergency," Gregory said.

His eyes held genuine appeal, she thought, but it was hardly the first time a patient had begged to use the telephone outside of calling times. She had to set boundaries, or else the whole structure would fall apart.

"I'm sorry, Michael. My answer is no," she repeated. "Now, it's nearly lunchtime. Why don't you go and find some of the others and have a game of table tennis, or something like that?"

He couldn't have said why that incensed him so much, but it probably had something to do with his hope that, on some visceral level, she would've been able to see he was not who he claimed to be. Which, of course, would have enabled them to have a genuine conversation, rather than her speaking to him as a five-year-old.

He weighed up everything he'd been told during his briefings with the FBI, versus everything he'd learned during his time at Buchanan Hospital. It was true that, in his view, there was a tendency for Doctor Kaufmann to rely more heavily on pharmacological interventions than was strictly necessary, but the opposite could be said of Doctor Palmer. Others might have tried to push antidepressants upon him, or other mood-altering drugs, but she'd focused on talking therapies in the first instance. That tended to be his own approach, which was not to say that there weren't cases where medicinal intervention was necessary; indeed, he knew of many cases where drugs had, quite literally, kept the patient alive. But those sorts of decisions were made on a case-by-case basis, with the benefit of a full medical history wherever possible—given that it had only been a couple of days, and she had nothing like that to hand, her caution was to her credit.

Bearing all of that in mind, he decided to trust her.

He had no choice.

"What I'm about to tell you is highly confidential," he said. "Do I have your word that you won't repeat it, to anyone?"

She frowned. "Michael, whatever you tell me in this room is protected by doctor-patient privilege."

"More than that," he replied. "This concerns the highest level of law enforcement, and the safety of one of your patients."

She said nothing, but moved across the room to sit in her usual chair.

"Sit down, Michael. I'm listening."

"This isn't a therapy session," he snapped, and then let out a frustrated breath. "Look, my name isn't Michael Jones. I'm here as part of an undercover operation with the FBI."

Her face remained impassive, and he knew that she didn't believe him. How could she? It sounded like one of the stories Harry would make up.

He ploughed on regardless.

"What operation would that be, Michael?"

He hesitated, but decided not to tell her the full details just yet.

"It concerns one of your patients," he said. "I was sent in here to find out whether they were really ill, and, if not, to find out why they were here. The FBI believes they may be in grave danger."

She steepled her fingers together and pressed them to her lips while she thought. She could guess which patient Michael was talking about—it was common knowledge that Lorena Romano was the wife of a notorious gangster who, much to her own personal displeasure, made weekly trips to the hospital, at which times he usually found some pretext upon which to make her feel uncomfortable.

Michael had been spending some time with Lorena lately, and it was possible he'd latched onto her, or what he saw as her glamorous, dangerous past. He was the son of a rich man, who'd never had a proper job—that kind of boredom could do funny things to the mind, particularly an intelligent mind, such as creating wild stories wherein he was cast as the hero of the tale, sent to rescue a damsel in distress.

Hardly original, she thought.

"Who is it you need to call?" she asked, deciding to let the fantasy play out.

"My contact at the FBI," he answered immediately. "Also, my friend and colleague, Professor Bill Douglas."

She almost laughed at that. Naomi had heard some wild delusions in her time, but nobody had claimed to be working with Professor William Douglas—a psychiatrist of worldwide renown—and taken the liberty of shortening his name to 'Bill'. This was more concerning to her than the Mafia story, because it showed that he'd done some research before his arrival at the Buchanan, which was the only explanation she could think of as to why he'd know Douglas's name. That demonstrated a certain premeditation to his actions and, given his actions the day before, she came to the sad conclusion that he was not only delusional, but untrustworthy.

None of this showed on her face.

"Look," he said. "You can google my name. *Doctor Alexander Gregory*."

It rang a bell, she thought. Probably some other well-known academic he'd looked up on the internet, and decided to impersonate.

"I don't need to do that," she said.

"You believe me, then? Thank God, I've been going out of my mind…"

You could say that, she thought.

"Look, Michael—"

"Alex."

She cleared her throat.

"Right. Sorry. *Alex*, I think the best thing would be for me to call up the FBI myself and confirm this with them, directly. You understand, I hear a lot of wild tales, doing the job I do."

Yes, he could understand.

Just as he could understand she didn't believe a single word he'd said.

LJ ROSS

"It's about Lorena," he said, urgently. "And my friend, Bill. I've been trying to call him for the past couple of days, but he's not picking up. I'm very worried."

"Can't you ask your cousin to help?"

"That's not my cousin," he said. "He's the FBI contact I was telling you about. Agent Hawk."

The fantasy kept growing, she thought. It was so elaborate, she was worried about the lengths he had gone to sustain it. For a patient to construct an entirely new fantasy world, whilst also being able to conduct life in the 'real' world well enough, they needed to have had significant practice at doing it.

Which made her think he'd been suffering from a personality disorder for years, and was in need of urgent intervention.

"Do you have his number?" she asked suddenly.

"Whose?"

"Hawk's," she said. "Let me call him, now. And your friend, Douglas. I'll dial the numbers."

She rose to walk around her desk, where she pressed the silent alarm.

Then, she picked up the telephone.

"Alright, which one first."

Relieved, Gregory hurried over.

"Let's try Bill, first."

He read out the number, which she dialled. She half-expected it to run through to some Chinese takeaway, but instead, it rang out.

"No answer," she said, and watched his face register concern.

"Still? This can't be good," he said. "Please, we need to call the hospitals around Washington DC—"

"DC?" she asked, incredulous. She was sure that Douglas was based somewhere in England—either Oxford or Cambridge. Next, he'd be telling her he had a line straight to the Oval Office.

"It's where Bill's staying," he said. "But we should try Hawk's number, first. He might have some news for me."

He rattled off the number and, again, she waited to hear a jingle of some kind.

Again, there was no answer.

"Shit," Gregory muttered, running his hands through his hair as he paced. "This is serious. If anything's happened to either or both of them, that could mean Paolo knows about Lorena."

They were back to the Mafia part of the story, she thought.

Fascinating case study.

"Look, you've got to ring the FBI main line and ask for Ellen Walker. She's Chief of BAU-5."

She glanced towards the door, and he caught it.

In that moment, he looked at her with such heartfelt disappointment, she might have believed he was actually telling the truth. But then, he believed he was.

"They're coming, aren't they?"

She didn't pretend to misunderstand.

"Yes, Michael. I'm here to help you, and you're experiencing a moment of crisis. Please let me try to help you through it."

A moment later, one of the larger nurses, Fletcher, burst into the room with a couple of others. They might have been expecting to find their usual kind of crisis patient; angry, aggressive, out of control.

But Gregory was none of these.

"I'll come quietly," he said, then turned back to Doctor Palmer with sad green eyes. "Please trust me enough to put the call through. Please, just do that much."

He was so earnest, she found herself agreeing.

CHAPTER 26

Gregory was escorted back to his room for observation by Fletcher and, soon after, Tilda arrived with a tray of food.

"Thought you might be hungry," she said.

He wasn't, but he appreciated the thought.

"Thanks."

"It's alright, Fletch, I've got it," she said, but the man hesitated and cast a suspicious eye over Gregory, who stood beside the window.

"Michael isn't going to do anything silly—*are you*, Michael?"

He stuck his hands in the pockets of the grey sweatpants Agent Hawk had provided for him, and shook his head.

"Like what? Pretend I'm working with the FBI, to try to get an extra phone call?"

Tilda pursed her lips, and set the tray down on top of his bed. He saw that she'd managed to procure one of Lorena's cannoli for him, and was touched by the small act of kindness.

She waited until Fletcher closed the door behind him, then perched on the edge of the bed to pour him some decaffeinated coffee. Caffeine was a regulated substance at Buchanan Hospital and, apparently, they'd determined his system didn't need any extra stimulation.

"Doctor Palmer tells me you've been having some"—she thought of the most diplomatic word to use—"*interesting* fantasies, Michael."

His lips twisted. "Does she? What else does the good doctor say?"

"Now, Michael," she said. "You came to us because you recognised something wasn't quite right and you needed help. Isn't it a good thing, when we do?"

Sure, he thought. It was great when a clinician was able to help their patient in the midst of a personal crisis. Except, it wasn't that kind of crisis. This was a case of life and death—and, to top it off, everyone thought he was losing his marbles.

As if he hadn't already lost them years ago, he thought.

"Here," she said, thrusting the coffee towards him.

He took the cup from her outstretched hand, and thought about whether he should do a study one day on the widespread benefits of the scent of fresh coffee—even decaf—on cognitive wellbeing.

He chugged back a couple of mouthfuls and instantly felt better.

"Do you want to talk about it?" Tilda asked, shaking the plate of cannoli to inveigle him. "I'm a good listener."

Gregory was in two minds about how to handle the situation. Deciding to risk telling Doctor Palmer about the reality of his position had backfired spectacularly, to the degree she now thought he was experiencing a psychotic episode—or, possibly, undiagnosed schizophrenia. During their next therapy session that afternoon, he expected her to tell him she'd like to prescribe a course of anti-psychotic medication and, without any external validation of his story, he didn't know how he'd be able to argue against it— other than forcibly refusing his consent.

"Have you ever felt trapped, Tilda?" he asked quietly. "As if you had nowhere left to run?"

She laughed, but it lacked its usual 'tinkle'.

"Of course I have," she said softly. "Everybody does sometimes, honey."

He gave in to temptation and took a bite of Lorena's excellent cannoli, thinking that, if he ever made it through this strange episode of his life, he'd come out half a stone heavier on the other side.

"Sometimes, our mind plays tricks," Tilda continued, and was pleased to see him eating. "It tells us things that aren't true, to make us feel better…"

He dusted his fingers off, and leaned back against the wall.

There was nothing he could tell her that wouldn't compromise Lorena, or himself, and the frustration was all-consuming.

"I guess you're right," he said, robotically.

Tilda clucked her tongue. "There's a social this evening," she said, changing tack. "If you're feeling up to it, you should come along."

He remembered Doctor Kaufmann mentioning something about a 'Sunday Social', where the staff and patients gathered together in the old ballroom for music and dancing. A sort of alternative therapy, he supposed.

He had no intention of dancing while his friend was somewhere out there, hurt or endangered, and no intention of letting his guard drop while an equally great threat loomed from within the hospital walls. For, if Bill Douglas had been targeted—and Agent Hawk likewise—there were only two other people presenting an obstacle to Paolo Romano.

Himself and Lorena.

Part of his greatest skill as a criminal profiler lay in his ability to understand offender behaviour and, in particular, being able to step into their minds to calculate likely behavioural patterns. Past experience played a big part in all this but, in that regard, he felt woefully inadequate; he'd researched gang culture in the United States and had devoured past case files made available to him by Agent Johnson, but he'd never followed a police investigation as he had in the UK, working with them to understand the ins and outs. It made it harder for him to predict how Paolo might react.

If Kaufmann was on the payroll, maybe he'd already ordered that Lorena be put to sleep, like Danny Barone.

Before learning of her treachery with the FBI, perhaps Paolo had wanted her to get well, but it would only take a phone call to change all that.

On the other hand, if Kaufmann wasn't on the payroll, and Paolo still wanted Lorena gone, he would have to send someone inside to take care of it. It would have to be a recent addition to the hospital…

Only one person matched that description.

Noah.

To get the job done, he'd need to orchestrate a moment when Lorena was unattended—it wouldn't take long, a woman of her size. Some nasty accident, or staged suicide… maybe neither, if the man was loyal to his boss and intended to take the fall for his crime. He'd need a moment when others were distracted…

Like a social.

Gregory turned back to Tilda with blazing green eyes.

"I'll be there," he said.

CHAPTER 27

Gregory could have sworn he smelled toffee.

Really strong caramel toffee; the kind they wrapped around apples at the fair.

He sniffed the air, drawing in a long breath to savour the scent of it.

"Michael?"

"Mmm?"

"Are you paying attention to our conversation?"

He turned to look at Doctor Palmer, who had flowers in her hair. He started to hum the Lumineers song of the same name.

"Michael, I'm concerned you're experiencing a psychotic break—"

"Yes, I know you are," he said, and grinned at her. "You're wondering if it's schizophrenia or some other disorder, and whether you should prescribe anti-psychotics."

She stared at him.

"I'm glad you can make light of this, but I see this as a very serious matter," she said. "Your ongoing health is a concern to me, and—"

"Did you call Agent Hawk?" he asked, suddenly remembering there was something important he meant to ask her.

Her lips firmed. "Yes, I called the number you gave me, and nobody answered—"

Gregory grinned again. "That's great. Really great."

She frowned. "What is?"

"That you called."

She sighed.

"Did you try Bill's number again?"

"Yes, Michael, I did, and it took me straight through to a rental car company in Baltimore."

He frowned, his face screwing up like a child's, as he tried to work out what might have happened.

"Must've had it in the car," he said.

"Had *what* in the car?"

"His mobile phone, of course. Must have had it in the glove compartment, or something, and the rental company found it. You need to call the hospitals, or the police. Or Ellen. Call Ellen Walker."

She tapped the edge of her pen against her notebook, feeling oddly emotional as she listened to him build on his fantasy with every new setback. When she'd first met him, Michael Jones had been sad, lonely…but she'd never suspected this.

Naomi felt that, by failing to spot his illness sooner, she'd failed him.

She looked away sharply, drawing herself in.

"I did call the FBI, Michael."

And what an embarrassing conversation that had been.

"I called their main line and they even checked with Chief Walker. She's never heard of Michael Jones."

"I'm not Michael," he reminded her, with a waggle of his index finger. "Remember?"

"I remember what you told me," she said, working hard to keep her patience. His behaviour had swung wildly from quiet withdrawal to childishness almost overnight.

"I've done everything you asked me, Michael. I even looked up Doctor Gregory online and, yes, I admit, there's a passing resemblance, which is probably why you subconsciously chose him as part of your internal fantasy—"

He began to laugh, long and hard, until tears came to his eyes. She waited until he subsided, then snapped her notebook shut.

"I'd like to recommend a course of anti-psychotics, alongside our continued sessions and more intensive cognitive behavioural therapy…"

The smell of toffee was back, he thought.

"I'm not taking any drugs," he said.

She watched him, saw the dilated pupils and flushed skin, and felt terribly sad. If it wasn't contraband drugs he'd managed to procure, somehow, then it was his own illness that had caused this heightened state.

"Are you sure? Is there anything you need to tell me?"

"Nope," he said. "Not telling you anything, anymore. Even if you have kind eyes. Especially because of that."

She felt a lump rise to her throat.

"You're—you're welcome to come to the social this evening," she said. "I hope you'll be in a better mood, after dinner."

Soon after, Tilda returned to collect him and Doctor Palmer remained seated, looking out of the windows across the lawn, which dipped low at the end, beyond which was a stone wall.

She found herself wondering if some walls were just too high to climb.

―――――――――

After his session with Doctor Palmer, Gregory had been overcome by tiredness and returned to his bedroom, where he'd fallen into a dead sleep, filled with lucid dreams bursting with colour and sound. When he awoke, he felt groggy and dehydrated, with a throbbing headache behind his eyes.

He stood in the shower for long minutes, flicking between hot and cold to wake himself up, and drank several pints of water. He thought about what Doctor Palmer had told him about her conversation with FBI and was unsurprised to learn she knew nothing of their particular mission; the sensitivity of the case meant Hawk and Johnson had been tasked to keep it within a very tight circle, on a 'need-to-know' basis. Although they'd formed part of the conference, the agents had their own case files to manage, part of which may include making deliberate omissions, if their orders came from the very top.

The immediate problem was still protecting Lorena and, to a lesser degree, himself. The stress had obviously been getting to him, judging by his exhaustion earlier, and he remembered he hadn't eaten very much that day. It was hardly surprising that his body had protested. He intended to fuel himself at dinner, but, until then, it was time to try Douglas's number again.

He glanced at the clock on the wall.

Quarter-to-four.

He made his way downstairs.

When he reached the calling room, he found Tilda and Doctor Kaufmann waiting for him.

"Ah, Mr Jones!"

Kaufmann welcomed him as though he were a long-lost relative, and was grinning so broadly, Gregory feared his face might crack.

"Good afternoon," he replied, politely. "I'd like to make a telephone call, please."

Kaufmann sucked in a breath, which hissed through his caps.

"Ah, now. I'm sorry to be the bearer of bad tidings, Michael, but Doctor Palmer and I feel it would be unhelpful for your recovery to allow outside calls at this time—"

Gregory continued to watch him, and Kaufmann was uncomfortable.

"I understand you've been experiencing some concerning delusions—"

"No."

The word was spoken calmly, and Kaufmann blinked.

"No?"

"I haven't been experiencing delusions," Gregory clarified. "Doctor Palmer is mistaken, and hasn't yet been able to corroborate my story, which has led her to believe it's part of a psychotic episode. It isn't, and allowing me to make a simple call or two should help to confirm it."

Kaufmann looked at Tilda, who raised an eyebrow.

"Very well," he said, expansively. "Let's see what evidence you can give us."

But, again, there was no answer for Douglas or Hawk, and it would be the early hours of the morning at Hawking College, Cambridge, so nobody would be around to answer Douglas's telephone there.

While Gregory racked his brain, the other two watched him with knowing smiles.

"I think that's quite enough," Kaufmann said, after another failed attempt to get through to Hawk. "Other patients are waiting to use the telephone, Michael."

Gregory felt the walls of the room begin to close in again, and panic rose like a tidal wave.

"You need to believe me," he said, tremulously. "I'm telling you the truth—"

"We know you are, Michael. We know you believe that."

"No! It's real, it's absolutely real!"

He made a sudden grab for the telephone again, and Kaufmann nodded to Tilda, who hurried off in search of Fletcher or one of the other orderlies.

"Michael," Kaufmann warned. "Calm yourself."

Gregory shoved the man away and grabbed the phone, punching in '911'.

Operator. What is your emergency?

There was a pause followed by silence, as the line was suddenly disconnected.

Gregory turned slowly to see three faces watching him, and let the telephone fall limply from his hand.

CHAPTER 28

By dinnertime, it was obvious the staff had been given instructions not to allow Gregory to be left to speak to Lorena alone. He was refused access to the kitchen, and firmly led away from her table to sit with Ira and Kitty, Noah having already taken up the fourth seat at his usual table with Harry, Marco and one of the other residents.

"Alexander!" Kitty exclaimed.

Tilda rolled her eyes. "Stay there," she told him sternly. "I'll go and get you a plate."

Kitty regarded him with a serene, sedated smile.

"You don't seem yourself today," she said. "Are you angry about Terrence?"

Gregory's fists curled beneath the table. He had no time for a chat about the woman's husband or why she'd felt it necessary to incinerate him, forty years ago.

He wanted to get to the telephone or, alternatively, to get the hell out of Dodge—preferably with Lorena.

His eyes slid over to where she was seated at a table on the other side of the room, nearest the nurses' station. She seemed happy, he thought, and he would be sorry to change that, but she must have known when she first entered the hospital that the stolen moments with her daughter would eventually come to an end. She must have planned her exit, somehow.

Tilda returned with a heaped plate of spaghetti and meatballs. "Eat up."

She seemed to hover for a moment, unsure whether she should stay beside him to make sure he followed through with that request, then she stepped away.

"I'll be on the nurses' table, Michael. Don't let me down."

"Tastes good," Kitty said, not looking up from the intricate task of winding her spaghetti around one of the hospital's bendy plastic forks. "Like they used to make it in *Sandro's*."

Gregory looked around the room and then settled on Noah, who was making animated conversation with Harry and Marco about sports, most likely. Already, he'd ingratiated himself with the other residents.

Jealous? his mother's voice whispered. *Did you think they were your friends?*

He rubbed the headache at his temple, and told himself to eat. He needed to stay strong.

While Gregory forked up a few mouthfuls, Ira mumbled to himself as he wound the largest mouthful of spaghetti he'd ever seen, and Kitty chattered about life in New York before 'everything changed'.

"You know, I remember, in the sixties we'd go for supper at *Copacabana*," she said. "They had all kinds of acts play there…Lucille Ball, Desi Arnaz…then, in the seventies, before Terrence passed, he'd take me along to *Studio 54* now and then. My goodness, it was hot in there, and the music was really *too* loud. Not like it used to be—"

Gregory set his fork down, feeling suddenly unwell.

He assumed it was the company, and reached for a glass of water. As he raised it to his lips, he paused to look inside, where the water swirled as though it were draining from a plughole. At the bottom was a tiny goldfish.

"Huh," he said, and set it back down on the table.

He looked across at Kitty, who wore a leopard-print scarf which she'd wound around her head in a glamorous turban of sorts. Gregory stared at it, eyes widening as the tail-end began to wag and curl, as if it were a real leopard.

But he wasn't afraid, and reached out a hand to touch it.

"Oh, do you like my scarf, dear? This was a present from an admirer of mine," Kitty said.

Gregory turned to Ira, whose spaghetti was now a swirling plate of worms, swimming in tomato sauce.

"Don't eat it," he told him, in a faraway voice. "Don't eat that."

He looked down at his hands, at the creases and curves, hardly noticing the tremors. His veins were swollen, and he heard the rush of blood, deafening as a waterfall.

He flexed them, fascinated by the way they moved.

"Are you alright, dear?"

He smiled over at Kitty.

"Yes, Mrs Steenberg. I need to call...there's someone I think I need to call."

"Oh, but the social's about to start," she complained. "Don't you want to dance with the pretty doctor?"

She winked at him.

Dance?

He never danced, but he'd like to.

"Has he come around yet?"

A doctor and nurse stood in a huddle at the end of Bill Douglas's hospital bed at Georgetown University Hospital.

"Just once, earlier today. Woke up, asking about somebody called 'Gregory'," the nurse said. "Told me I needed to call Buchanan Hospital about it."

The doctor ran a tired hand over his face. Ten straight hours was beginning to take a toll.

"Buchanan...you mean the place up in the Catskills? It's a psychiatric facility—"

The nurse nodded.

"I called them, to ask if they had anybody there called 'Gregory'. The receptionist told me they don't have anybody by that name."

The doctor looked down at Douglas, who was now sleeping.

"Who d'you reckon he was talking about? His son?"

"Not according to his friends," she said. "They say he probably meant some guy called Alexander Gregory, who's a friend of his. They said he's travelling the East Coast, but they don't know anything about the Buchanan, and they don't have a number for him."

"He must've been confused, poor guy. You can hardly blame him, after what he's been through. Maybe when the Professor wakes up again, he can try calling his friend," the doctor said.

"Yeah, it's probably not important."

They left, to continue their rounds.

———

Paolo was feeling philosophical, that night.

The small pizzeria and live music bar he owned a few streets away from his home was filled with people, every one of them a made man. Tony, his underboss, then Franco and Matteo—two of his *caporegime*. Then there was his son, Luca, and his two elder brothers, Vincenzo—named for his grandfather—and Gabriele.

There was Andy, too, if he was in the mood to be generous.

They were all handsome boys, who got their looks from Lorena, and everything else from him.

Lorena.

Even thinking of her made him want to kill something.

A band of three played classic Italian music, but the lead singer's voice was mostly drowned out by the sound

LJ ROSS

of raucous laugher and Vincenzo's loud-mouthed stories about the women he'd banged that week. He'd always been the loudest of the three, Paolo thought, and the bravest. He would be a worthy successor, some day, when he retired.

It was a shame Lorena wouldn't be around, but that was her own damn fault.

"How's it goin', boss?" Tony ambled over and sat down heavily on one of the wooden chairs next to him, already half drunk.

Paolo looked at his old friend, then back at the room.

"Everythin's taken care of," he said quietly.

"What's taken care of, Pop?"

Luca was seated across the table with Janey on his lap. Paolo was glad to see his son had taken his constructive advice on that score; it would've been a shame to have to enforce it.

"Go get us some more beers, sweetheart," he told her. Once Janey had sashayed over to the bar, Paolo turned back to Luca. "I already told you," he said. "We don't talk business in front of the women."

"Sorry, Pop."

"S'alright, you're still learnin' these things, but listen to me," Paolo said, slurring a bit. "When some little honey's had her hands on you, she'll make you think anythin's okay, but it ain't. You remember that."

Luca nodded, and waited to see if his father would confide in him which, eventually, he did.

"Another thing you need to learn is how to send a message. Y'understand?"

"What, you mean like the old way?"

Paolo nodded. "Different times, different problems," he said, still watching the room. "Take your mother, for example."

"Ma? What about her? I thought she was doin' better."

"Yeah, that's what we all thought, kid," Tony put in, with a snort.

One look from Paolo silenced him.

"What's the most important thing in our family, Luca? Above all else?"

"Loyalty," his son answered, without having to think. It had been drummed into him, almost as soon as he could walk.

"And what do we do with those who are disloyal?"

"We punish them, Pop."

Luca paused to take a sip of his beer, already understanding where the conversation was headed. He tried to keep his expression neutral, tried to hide his horror in the face of a monster.

"You're goddamn right, we do," Tony said, banging the bottom of his beer bottle on the table to reinforce the sentiment.

"What if I told you your mother had betrayed the Family—betrayed us all, betrayed *me*?"

Luca looked him dead in the eye.

"I'd tell you she deserved all she got, and I'd help you make sure she did."

Paolo nodded slowly.

"Good kid."

CHAPTER 29

The ballroom had been set up like an old-time supper club.

It may not have been up there with *Copacabana,* but the hospital had done the best it could. The old chandeliers gave off a dim, fizzing light that reflected in the mirrored panels around the room, lending a warm, sepia hue to their Sunday Social. Petit-fours and pitchers of non-alcoholic cocktails stood on a side table, while Doctor Kaufmann took turns with Harry to play on the antique Bechstein in the corner, or choose a record for the gramophone beside it. There were no loudspeakers or hard, thumping music. Everything was soft, and easy on the disordered mind.

Which was fortunate, Gregory thought, because his was wildly out of whack.

The awareness that he'd been drugged, probably with some kind of hallucinogen, hit him around the same time as he spotted the goldfish in the bottom of his water glass. It was less terrifying than he'd imagined it would be, because the experience came with a certain stoicism;

there was little he could do about it, now, so he might as well enjoy the ride. He'd learned that it was possible to experience the hallucinations whilst also continuing to appear normal—or, rather, as close an approximation as he could muster. He saw the dancing imps across the ballroom, acknowledged them as not being real, and then tried to focus on something else.

Unconsciously, he'd done his usual trick of positioning himself near to the door, leaning a shoulder against the wall while he watched the other residents dancing around to the honky-tonk music Harry was treating them to. He was processing the fact that the floor appeared to be moving as though they were on water, when Doctor Palmer crossed the room to speak to him.

He tried not to notice the smoke trail she left on the floor.

"Hello, Michael. I'm glad you've joined us," she said.

There was a caution in her voice that he was sorry for, but he could hardly blame her. Right now, he was seeing musical notes in the air.

"Wouldn't miss it," he muttered, keeping half an eye on where Lorena was standing chatting to Rosie and Tilda.

"How are you feeling?"

Oh, no, he thought.

He wouldn't be making that mistake again.

"We aren't in a therapy session at the moment," he said.

She nodded, and looked around the room.

"Don't you want to mingle with the others? You might find something in common."

"I have something in common with you," he said.

"Oh?" she said coolly. "What might that be?"

"Rhythm."

She couldn't help but smile. "Most men wouldn't claim to have rhythm," she said. "That's quite a bold statement."

"I'm feeling bold."

She was caught off-guard. "Michael, I—"

"Doctor Kaufmann's dancing with Kitty, I see," Gregory pointed out. "Some of the other nurses are dancing with patients. Isn't that the point of the Social? To mingle on a social level?"

"Well, yes, I suppose."

He turned to her, eyes shining beneath the light of the chandelier.

"In that case, would you like to dance with me?"

Yes, she thought.

"I don't think it would be appropriate," she said.

"For whom?"

She swallowed. To answer that would be to admit she had even entertained anything other than a professional regard for him, as her patient.

"It's a general rule of mine, not to dance with the patients."

He smiled his lop-sided smile. "Coward," he whispered.

Her chin lifted. "Alright then," she said. "One dance won't hurt."

The music had changed to something smooth and lilting, a melody he didn't recognise but would later learn was one of

Harry's own compositions. He and Naomi swayed together, their bodies in time, their eyes meeting—but they never touched, although others were unafraid to.

"See? I don't bite," he said.

"Michael—"

"Please, stop calling me that."

"It's your name," she said softly.

"Not anymore."

She didn't argue the point, acknowledging instead that there had been a yearning inside her for just one moment like this with him. A taste of what it might have been like, she supposed, if things had been different.

Except they weren't different.

He was her patient, and that was all.

There was a quality to him that was both frightening and exciting; something she'd been warned about since the earliest days of her clinical experience.

Don't be drawn in, they'd said. *Don't allow personal feelings to cloud your judgment,* they'd said.

Remember your professional obligations.

The words ran around her mind in time to the sway of the music, until she stopped and stood still.

"That's enough," she said, more to herself than to him.

Gregory nodded. "Thank you," he said.

The light bounced off the mirrors behind her, and made it appear that she stood against a backdrop of stars. Even if it was a hallucination—all of it, even the dancing— he hoped his mind would allow him to remember it.

CHAPTER 30

Gregory couldn't see Lorena.

He turned this way and that, seeking her out amongst the patients who moved awkwardly around the room, heads lolling, arms flailing—some spinning like children. There were often dance nights at Southmoor, which he attended more out of a sense of duty, to put the patients at their ease and close the gap between 'them' and 'us'. But, inevitably, it was an awkward coupling of patients and staff, where those who were classified as 'unwell' met those somewhere else on the same scale, albeit without a DSM diagnosis to mark the distinction. Their eccentricities and, often, lack of social skills, made the occasion fraught with the potential for drama and, were it not for the obvious pleasure it gave the residents, he might have questioned its utility.

But, at the Buchanan, he'd found himself part of that eccentric, awkward crowd of jittering, drooling, hallucinating, stammering or silent unfortunates, and knew now what it was to feel the dark side of the moon.

He'd experienced the crushing humiliation wrought by a pitying look, a sidelong glance, or…

Or the rejection of a lovely woman, who thought him mad.

Humans were essentially social creatures, with a need to find friendship, companionship, or a tribe they could call their own. That was never more true than when he looked around the ballroom at Buchanan Hospital, where he saw Ira and Kitty performing a slow cha-cha, while Marco turned the pages of Harry's music book, and Megan sat on the edge of the floor with Rosie, who read to her. Naomi was dancing in a group with some of the other patients, laughing with them, while Kaufmann spoke to a huddle of nurses on the edge of the floor. There was companionship here, even in the depths of despair.

But there was still no Lorena.

A movement beside the door caught his eye, and he saw Noah slipping out of the room.

If Paolo had chosen to send in one of his own to silence Lorena, that young man presented the most likely candidate. Even now, he could be searching the corridors for his mark, while she thought herself safe from the outside world.

Gregory made a beeline for the door.

———

Gregory struggled to keep up with Noah, who'd taken off somewhere along the corridors of the hospital. His head felt too heavy for his body, the music of the ballroom sounding distant and warped as his feet tripped over the parquet floor towards the main hallway. He ignored the hands that waved to him from the paintings that lined the walls, and the overpowering stench of rotting flesh which seemed the grow stronger as he left his tribe behind him.

He saw a figure dart across the hallway up ahead, and he stumbled onward, stomach rolling, head swimming, to catch them.

But when he reached the hallway, there was nobody there.

Michael.

He heard his mother's voice and turned too quickly, falling to the floor.

Here I am, Michael.

He saw the shadow stop beside the front desk and, just for a moment, it took his mother's shape and form.

"She's dead," he whispered. "You're hallucinating."

But the figure remained, rattling the door behind the reception desk.

Gregory rose to his feet again, pushing himself onward, knowing he needed to stop whoever was planning to hurt Lorena.

As he drew nearer, the figure turned, and he saw the metallic sheen of a pocket blade gripped tightly in a fist.

"I wasn't doing anything," Noah whispered, flipping the blade shut again. "See? I'm not trying to hurt anybody."

"What are you planning to do with that knife?" Gregory asked.

"Look, just drop it," Noah said, rubbing his mouth. "Just turn around and go away."

"I can't do that," Gregory said. "I know why you're here."

He thought he saw confusion pass over the man's face, but he couldn't be sure. Night had fallen, and there was only the frugal glow of the old Victorian wall lights to guide his way.

"Look, man, I was only going to take a couple of vials—"

Now, it was Gregory who was confused.

"Do you really have to tell anybody about this? I managed three months clean, last year, but it's been tough this time around…"

Gregory looked at the plaque on the door where Noah stood, which read, 'MEDICINES', then back at the flaxen-haired man who stood shaking and sweating beside it.

"You wanted drugs," he realised.

"Well—yeah," Noah said. "What the hell did you think I was doing?"

Gregory shook his head, trying to think.

There was no sign of Lorena, and the man hadn't tried to hurt him; in fact, he looked grateful to have been interrupted.

"Did you see anybody else around?" he asked.

"No, they're all in the ballroom," Noah replied. "Why? What's wrong?"

But Gregory had already turned away, having realised where Lorena must be.

The kitchen.

Naomi poured herself a glass of 'Pineapple Punch', which consisted solely of pineapple juice and a dash of low-sugar lemonade, and looked around the ballroom. There were around thirty people gathered there, a couple of the staff who lived off-site having already excused themselves for the night. Those who lived on-site, like herself, had remained to supervise the patients.

She checked her watch.

Nine o'clock.

Still early, in the 'real' world, but getting late for the residents.

She tried to catch Kaufmann's eye, but he was otherwise engaged chatting to some of the younger nursing staff—regaling them with tales of his superior 'mind-reading' skills, no doubt. For the last year or more, Naomi had been wondering whether it was time to move on from the hospital and find somewhere she could really make an impact, rather than forever having to flatter and fluff a man who'd long since stopped caring about patient development and spent more of his time trying to figure out how many more beds they could squeeze onto the wards.

More beds, more money.

It was unlike her to feel so jaded, and she tried to find something more uplifting to focus her attention on. There was Harry and Marco, for starters; two men who were nothing and everything alike, born to different mothers, but who could have been brothers. They'd fought like cat and dog, the first week or two they'd known one another—but, since then, it had been plain sailing for the most part.

Then, there was Lorena.

She'd made incredible progress over the past month, and especially during the past week. Naomi had known there was some deep, underlying trauma Lorena needed to confront, but it hadn't been until their group session the previous day that they'd finally had a breakthrough. In truth, she had Michael to thank, in part. His openness during their group sessions was extraordinary in comparison with other new admissions, and had helped other members of the group to talk more openly, too.

She looked for both of them, but couldn't see either.

Naomi set her glass down and looked more closely, then frowned.

Tilda was missing, too.

CHAPTER 31

Gregory ran as quickly as he could, feet skidding over the polished floor as he fought to control his wayward limbs. His mind was still not fully his own and there was no doubt he'd been drugged. The only surprising thing was how long it had taken him to figure out who'd been responsible.

In the seconds it took him to race along the corridor to the kitchen, he replayed the events of the day, tracking his own symptoms.

He'd started to see flowers and smell toffee when he'd had his session with Doctor Palmer after lunch.

The lunch Tilda had served him, in his room, shortly before.

Afterwards, he'd been exhausted and dehydrated, with a raging headache. Then, later, he'd seen goldfish and leopard tails over dinner.

The dinner Tilda had served him.

On the dance floor, as he'd forgotten himself and stolen a dance with Doctor Palmer, he remembered seeing Tilda talking to Lorena, as they'd stacked the empty plates to take back to the kitchen.

He remembered now that Paolo Romano had greeted Tilda personally and as a final, damning piece of evidence, she had also been Danny Romano's 'key nurse' during his stay at Buchanan Hospital. He'd seen it, in the file he'd pilfered from Doctor Palmer's office.

Paolo Romano hadn't needed to send anybody inside to murder his wife, Gregory realised, because he already had somebody ready and waiting. All the time Lorena had been a patient, Tilda had probably been feeding information back to her husband and, so long as everybody believed she was really ill, she remained safe.

But then, he'd come along and changed all that.

He was to blame.

Terrified, breathing hard, Gregory arrived at the kitchen door.

It was locked.

It was one area that was protected for safety reasons, and required key card entry.

Feeling sweat run down the small of his back, he shoved at it a couple of times, but it wouldn't budge. However, unlike the maximum-security wards, where the doors were reinforced, the kitchen door was made of heavy oak with the addition of an electronic mechanism. Difficult, but not impossible to break.

He didn't hesitate, but gave it everything he had, kicking at the wood until he heard a splintering sound and it swung open.

The lights were off in the kitchen when he entered, and there was only the neon glow of an energy-saving strip light to provide any illumination. The wide, square space was kitted out to restaurant standard, with long, stainless steel benches and range cookers. Knives and other dangerous implements were locked away religiously every night. On the other side of the room was a walk-in pantry.

The pantry.

He heard the thunder of footsteps down the corridor outside, so he wasted no time and raced across to the wide metal door, yanking it open.

Tilda's head snapped around.

The muscles in her arms were bunched and taut, glistening with the effort of holding the two ends of the kettle cord around Lorena's neck as she struggled beneath her, the stench of flour and sugar mingling with sweat as they fought a silent battle.

Gregory acted swiftly.

He grabbed the back of Tilda's hair, taking a fistful to yank her away sharply, thrusting her away from Lorena's now unconscious body. She stumbled as he did, and he watched with renewed horror as the side of her head connected with the edge of a steel countertop with a sickening *crunch.*

He turned back to Lorena and was in the process of unwinding the cord when he heard the door open again behind him.

"Michael...oh, God. What have you done?"

He turned to find Naomi looking at him with wide, frightened eyes, her face a picture of abject revulsion.

"No—no, this wasn't me—"

She stepped away to allow Fletcher and two more orderlies to enter, and the last thing Gregory remembered was the sharp scratch of a needle against his neck.

Then, nothing.

———

The call came through just before eleven.

Paolo swore volubly, and reached across a woman's naked backside to pick up his phone.

"What?"

It was Tony, at the other end. "I just had a call from our guy at the Medical Center, up in the Catskills," he said.

"Oh, yeah? Can I start grievin' yet, or what?"

Paolo traced an idle hand over the woman's skin, as he thought of how to celebrate his wife's unfortunate suicide.

"It's bad news, boss."

Paolo's hand fell away. "Give it to me."

"The nurse—Tilda, or whatever—was interrupted. She was hurt bad, too. They took her to the Emergency Room down in Harris," he said, referring to a town further south of Overlook Mountain.

Paolo swore again, and the woman beside him gave up on sleep to pad naked to the en suite bathroom next door.

"Lorena's still alive?" he asked, once she'd left.

"Yeah," Tony said. "At least, far as we know. She hasn't been admitted anywhere."

Paolo ran a hand over his gelled hair—or what was left of it.

"Alright, Tony. Make contact and tell them, okay, they win. We'll deal."

"You got it, boss."

Soon after his underboss rang off, Paolo received another call, this time from Doctor Kaufmann at Buchanan Hospital. It was to tell him his wife had been attacked by a fellow patient, but she was still alive, and had been seen by a doctor from the nearby clinic in Woodstock. Her larynx was bruised and her voice would be affected for a while, but she was fortunate to be otherwise unharmed, thanks to the early intervention of one of their nurses, Tilda.

Paolo listened and made all the right noises, saying he'd travel straight up to see her, as soon as he could. In ordinary circumstances, he'd have driven up there that same night to bring her home, but these weren't ordinary circumstances.

At least he didn't need to worry about them linking Tilda to any of it, he thought. They were pinning it on whichever dumbass went in there and stopped her, so he couldn't have set it up better, himself.

He rang off and, when his mistress wandered back into the room, he was laughing.

"Whassamatter wit' you?"

He patted his lap.

"C'mere baby, and I'll tell you."

CHAPTER 32

The next morning, everything had changed.

Gregory was no longer in the bedroom he'd grown used to, with its picturesque views of the Hudson Valley. He found himself strapped to a different bed altogether, in a room on the 'high-risk' ward of the Hudson Wing. Apart from the occasional suicide risk, or a particularly bad psychotic episode, it was an area seldom used at the Buchanan—its patients falling into the comfortable, reasonably well-adjusted categories of 'low' or 'medium' risk.

His body ached all over, and his throat was parched, but by far the worst pain came from not knowing how he'd come to be moved into the minimalist, white-washed space with its single, heavily-barred window and furnishings that were no longer antique but hospital-issue, and bolted to the floor, just like the toilet.

There was a CCTV camera high in the corner of the room, trained on the bed.

Somebody must have been monitoring him, because, within a matter of minutes, Doctor Palmer entered with Doctor Kaufmann at her side, as well as Fletcher, the security nurse.

Naomi had been up for most of the night, unable to come to terms with the escalation in his behaviour. She'd gone back over her notes of their sessions, unravelling and unpicking every word he'd said to try to understand what she'd missed, but nothing stood out.

She'd tried to prepare herself to face him again; to face the man she'd danced with, that she'd thought of...

It didn't matter now.

It would be a hard lesson for her to learn, but she'd learned it.

They all had.

"Good morning, Michael."

Her voice was entirely neutral, Gregory thought, and as flat as her eyes.

"Why have you put me in here?" he asked, and his voice was little more than a dry rasp.

Kaufmann nodded to Fletcher, who moved across to undo the straps holding him down, and hold out a plastic glass of water.

"Drink this," he said.

"What's in it?" Gregory asked, no longer willing to accept any food or drink without checking its origin.

"It's water," Naomi snapped. "That's all."

He gave her a mild look.

"I was drugged by an employee of this hospital—not once, but twice yesterday. I'm now suffering from withdrawal effects, so I have every right to ask."

They'd taken a blood sample from him the previous evening, she thought, but the results hadn't been returned. Even if he did have illegal drugs running around his system, it was ridiculous to accuse one of the staff of spiking his food.

"You're being held in one of our maximum-security rooms for your own protection, as well as that of the other residents," she said. "We've tried to contact your cousin to make him aware of the situation, but we've been unable to reach him, as yet. We'll keep trying."

Gregory said nothing, but sat up in the hard-sprung bed, wincing as the pain of having been wrestled to the ground the previous evening sang through his body. At least his head felt clearer than it had for the past twenty-four hours.

"How's Lorena?" he asked. "Is she recovering from her attack?"

The three clinicians looked at one another, and then turned to him with comic expressions of confusion and dismay.

"Your attack upon Tilda and Lorena have left both women badly hurt," Doctor Kaufmann said. "Tilda suffered a severe head injury and has been taken to hospital, whilst Mrs Romano suffered damage to her larynx and is recovering here. Do you feel any remorse for your actions, Michael? Is there anything you'd like to say?"

Gregory was incredulous.

"Just a minute," he said, growing agitated. "You—you think that *I'm* the one who attacked those women?"

They said nothing, only continued to look at him in silent dismay.

"For God's sake, won't you *listen*?" he cried. "I've already told you, I'm here because the FBI asked me to check on the status of their witness, Lorena Romano. She's planning to give evidence against her husband, Paolo, and they wanted to know why she didn't turn up at their pick-up, but instead wound up here, at Buchanan—"

"Michael, that's enough," Naomi said, wearily. "I've already tried calling the FBI, and nobody knows what you're talking about."

"What about Douglas?" he said, still desperately worried for his friend. "Please, did you try the hospitals?"

"We won't be entertaining your fantasies any longer," Kaufmann said. "They're clearly very damaging to you, and to others."

"Why don't you ask Lorena!" he cried. "Ask her, and she'll tell you all about Agent Hawk and Agent Johnson!"

"Even if we were remotely inclined to do so, Lorena couldn't answer us at the moment, because she's under sedation while she recovers." Kauffman replied, in even tones. "She's suffered terrible trauma, at your hands, Michael, and we wouldn't insult her, or her husband, by giving credence to the rumours surrounding their family."

"*Rumours*?" Gregory laughed. "Are you kidding me?"

He ran shaking hands over his hair, then his face, as he tried to think…to stay calm while the rest of the world went stark, raving mad.

"Alright," he said. "You won't ask her about that, then at least ask her to confirm I wasn't the one wrapping a cord around her throat. That was Tilda."

Naomi looked emotional, he thought, but for all the wrong reasons.

"Michael, please…just rest, and try to think over what you've done. We'll come and talk to you again, soon."

The door closed shut behind them, followed by the electronic *click* of an automatic door locking system. In the corridor outside, Kaufmann turned to his young colleague.

"I know that was hard for you," he said. "It's hard for all of us. You weren't the only one who believed that young man was on the road to recovery, but it just goes to show how much can reveal itself in a short space of time—"

"Lorena wouldn't necessarily know who attacked her, would she?" Naomi muttered.

"What d'you mean?"

"I mean, somebody—Michael—attempted to strangle her from behind," she said. "How would she know who it was, if they took her unawares?"

Kaufmann let out a disbelieving laugh.

"Naomi, we were all there to see what happened," he said. "I've never seen such a picture of guilt."

She nodded reluctantly, and thought of Tilda, the poor woman she'd known for three years as a dedicated, caring individual who was now battling to recover from a serious head injury.

"You're right," she said. "I was clutching at straws."

CHAPTER 33

The Commission hadn't met in ten years, not since they'd needed to discuss the question of the Albanian gangs, who'd made an organised attempt to infiltrate their turf in Westchester.

It had been created by Charles "Lucky" Luciano following the murder of Salvatore Maranzano, who'd declared himself *capo di tutti capi*, or the 'boss of all bosses', back in the early 1930s—a title which emboldened Maranzano to demand each of the other crime bosses from the Five Families pay him for the privilege. Following his murder, Lucky Luciano had decided on a better, more equitable arrangement for all, which also made him less of a target to other ambitious men. He'd set up the Commission along business lines, with a board of directors made up of the bosses of the most powerful families across the country who met every five years or so, to discuss how to govern the United States.

Nowadays, the Commission had reduced its membership to a more exclusive circle, consisting of seven family bosses, including the Five Families of New York, the Romano Family of New Jersey and the Chicago Outfit. Back in the thirties, Luciano had presided as chairman, but that honour now fell to Paolo Romano.

However, that day, the Commission met in secret, without its chairman.

The meeting was held on Genovese territory, near the old Meatpacking District of New York. The place had undergone a total overhaul over the past century, and was now the province of upmarket factory and warehouse renovations that sold for millions at a time, trendy hotels and restaurants part-owned by musicians and artists. On this occasion, they'd foregone their usual refinements in favour of meeting in the part-constructed interior of one of Genovese's apartment projects, which afforded them adequate privacy and a two-way exit strategy, should the need arise.

Secrecy was paramount, with each man bringing just one bodyguard.

Folding chairs were provided, but that was all.

Arturo DiAngelo was a sprightly man of seventy-five, and the current boss of the Lucchese Family. Having previously been one of the most powerful of all, he was greeted with respect by the other bosses, who embraced one another and exchanged the usual crocodile-faced expressions of delight at having been reunited.

"Is he here, yet?" Arturo asked his second-in-command.

"Yes, boss. He's waiting in his car outside."

"Ask him in, but tell him to come alone. If he refuses, tell him there's no trust between us."

He didn't care if the kid was his grandchild, Arturo thought. He was also his father's son.

"You asked us here, Arturo, and we came," the Genovese boss began. "Our meeting is not on neutral ground, but on my territory, as you requested. For you, Arturo, and for the sake of our long friendship, I agreed to this."

The other bosses slapped their knees in support.

"Now, I see our chairman is missing," Genovese continued, with a gleam in his eye. "Can you explain this?"

Arturo spread his hands. "Friends, brothers, you remember how things used to be, before the New Jersey War. The Families each had a stake, and there was no bloodshed."

"Those were good days," the Bonnano boss said. "But that was thirty years ago, and things are not the same. We are Six Families, now."

But Arturo heard the unspoken question, saw the glimmer of hope in his eyes, and knew he hadn't been alone in his resentment.

"Gentlemen, we are peace-loving men," he said, without any irony whatsoever. "Vincenzo Romano changed the natural order, and set Family against Family, after a decade of peace. His son has profited from that, these past thirty years."

"And married your daughter, Arturo," Genovese pointed out.

He placed his hands together in a parody of prayer. "It was my greatest hope that it would heal the wounds of the past," he said. "But now, we face a new crisis."

They heard approaching footsteps echoing against the concrete floor, and watched another man approach their small circle.

He walked alone and unprotected.

"Like father, like son," Genovese laughed. "Eh, Luca?"

Luca Romano stood with his arms outstretched, allowing the families' representatives to search him, so they could be satisfied he wasn't carrying.

Then, he came to stand beside his grandfather, declining the offer of a seat.

"My grandson has some information which may be of interest to all of us," Arturo said. "I need not tell you, he comes to tell us at great personal risk to himself."

"And yet, he comes to betray his father?" the Gambino boss said.

"He comes to right the wrongs of many years ago," Arturo corrected him. "I ask you to listen, that's all."

Luca's hands were clammy and his stomach rolled, but his resolve never wavered and he proceeded to set out his plan.

At the end, the bosses looked amongst one another, and one by one, they smiled.

"Have a seat, kid," one of them said. "You've earned it."

Gregory had always wondered what it would feel like to spend a night in a cell.

He'd wondered, whilst at the same time basking in the comfortable knowledge that it would never come to pass.

There was a well-worn saying that 'ignorance was bliss', a maxim to which he'd never fully ascribed, but, after spending the past few hours pacing within the four walls of his room, he was prepared to change his position on both fronts. It was another of life's little quirks that the high-risk, maximum-security cell in which he'd been left to rot had the same kind of Scandinavian-inspired décor one might find at one of the upscale chalet hotels further up the mountain. Apparently, hospital chic was *de rigueur*.

His only visitor had been Fletcher, who delivered meals which Gregory returned untouched, until Doctor Palmer appeared late in the afternoon with Fletcher by her side, for security.

"How are you feeling, Michael?"

She looked tired, he thought, and was sorry to have been the cause.

"Better, now that whatever Tilda gave me has worked its way out of my system," he said.

Naomi looked at him, and she had to admit his eyes looked considerably clearer than before, but she disputed the means by which he managed to procure whatever LSD-type substance had been swimming around his system.

"Tilda's likely to recover, in case you're wondering," she said.

"Good," he shot back. "That means she'll be fit to stand trial."

Naomi turned away in frustration, then spun back again.

"Why, Michael? Why did you attack her?"

She'd gone over and over it in her mind, but couldn't understand his motivations. Within Michael's internal fantasy world, he'd cast Lorena as a victim, and himself as a hero. He'd wanted to save her from the clutches of her Mafia family, apparently acting at the behest of the FBI. Setting aside the grandiose nature of his fabricated world, one thing stood out: he wanted to save Lorena, not to hurt her.

Which was why she couldn't understand what had changed for him, unless he was suffering from a more severe form of psychosis than she'd previously thought.

"I didn't attack her," he said, wearily. "Ask her, when she comes around."

"Lorena was attacked from behind," Naomi said. "She wouldn't be able to confirm or deny anything."

"No, but she'll be able to confirm her relationship with the FBI," he said, bullishly.

"Michael, I—" She shook her head, as though she couldn't stomach any more. "I came to tell you, the decision has been taken to transfer you into Doctor Kaufmann's primary care. Obviously, I missed something important during our sessions together and, for that, I want to apologise to you, and to all the people you've hurt. It was an oversight on my part, and it almost cost lives."

She looked at him with a mixture of regret and sadness.

"I'm sorry I couldn't help you, Michael."

"You did," he said. "More than you know, Naomi—but not in the way that you mean."

She tried to search his face for clues, tried to see the signs of his delusion, then gave up trying.

"Goodnight, Michael. Try to get some sleep."

CHAPTER 34

Another twenty-four hours passed while Gregory roamed the floor of his room, torturing himself thinking of what might have happened to his friend, and what may yet happen to the woman lying in Overlook Wing, weak and vulnerable to whichever assassin may be sent in to finish the job Tilda began.

Escape seemed to be his only option now, since honesty had failed him, but as his mind ran through the possible ways to achieve it, each seemed less plausible than the last. Unlike the floors below, the high-security ward of Hudson Wing was equipped with reinforced metal doors, albeit sporting the same porthole windows and wooden facing, to give the impression of equality between the wards. Added to which, the door was locked using the same central electronic system, which meant he would not be able to use brute force to break through it, as he had with the kitchen downstairs.

The single window in the room was a small dormer; large enough to afford a view, and prevent any accusations of cruelty, but small enough to prevent a grown man from trying to squeeze himself through, even if the outside bars had been absent.

Which they weren't.

There was no handy air vent, or ceiling access for him to exploit, nor any convenient waste access big enough for him to use in a kind of homage to *The Shawshank Redemption*. The room was, unfortunately, very secure, and afforded him very little chance of ever getting out without the hospital's approval.

Gregory slid to the floor, and stared at the white wall opposite.

How complacent he'd been, he thought. How unutterably *smug*, to think himself so untouchable. He'd built his stone wall, erected his gates and locked them tight, telling himself that they would be enough to keep him safe from the world.

How wrong he'd been.

There were no guarantees that all he'd built couldn't be torn down in a single moment, by a single person. There were no safeguards to protect his heart from the pain of love or loss—but to live the kind of half-life he'd been living was no life at all.

He thought of the people who'd loved him, and of how careless he'd been with their hearts—and how cowardly he'd been with his own.

He promised himself that, if tomorrow came, he would be brave.

Until then, he'd sleep, and dream of nothing.

The call came through shortly before ten o'clock.

Naomi was seated at her desk typing up her reports for the day when the phone rang. As the 'doctor on duty' that evening, external calls were routed through to her office from the front desk, so she tried to inject a bit of enthusiasm when she answered.

"Buchanan Hospital," she said.

"Hi there, my name's Eliza Wong, I'm a doctor at Georgetown University Hospital. Can I speak with the manager, please?"

Naomi was surprised. Their new admissions generally came from the Tri-State area, not from somewhere as far south as DC.

"I'm Doctor Palmer," she said. "I'm the duty manager this evening."

"Great, maybe you can help me?"

"I will, if I can, Doctor Wong. Do you have a patient you'd like to transfer for admission?"

"No, it's not that. We have an in-patient here who's recovering from a hit-and-run car accident—the guy's been in and out of it for the past few days, but he keeps going on about the same thing, whenever he comes around."

"What's that?"

"He keeps asking us to call you about some guy he knows—"

Just then, they were interrupted by the piercing wail of the hospital's fire alarm.

Naomi swore.

"I'm sorry, I have to go—we've got a situation here."

She ended the call and hurried out into the hallway, where the alarm was even louder, reverberating around the hospital walls with an ear-splitting metallic shriek.

Smoke was beginning to gather, clouding the air with the scent of burning wood, and she coughed, already feeling it clog the back of her throat.

The other evening staff converged in the hallway.

Where? Where is it?

I can't tell where it's coming from—

"Evacuate!" Naomi ordered. "Get everybody out!"

Gregory had been lying on his bed, half-asleep, when the alarm went off.

He leapt off the bed, instantly awake, and hurried to the door.

It remained locked.

Smoke leaked beneath the door and through its cracks, slowly but inexorably filling the room. He tugged at the door, banging against the heavy metal to be heard.

"Hey! Is anybody there? Open the door!"

He spun around, but already knew there was no other way out.

Desperately, he made another attempt to rip one of the side tables from the floor, kicking at the metal plate holding it there, intending to use it to break the window.

It wouldn't budge.

He tried every piece of furniture in the room, then went back to the door, shouting and banging to attract attention. Coughing, his eye fell on the small porcelain sink, and he used the heel of his foot to kick at it, working it free from the wall to use as a battering ram.

Then, the room was plunged into darkness.

Naomi had just turned the central unlocking key, when the lights suddenly went out.

She heard shrieks from some of the other staff, and the distant cries of patients hammering to be freed from their rooms, as black smoke gathered all around.

Just then, Kaufmann burst out of his office, carrying an armful of files.

"What the hell are you doing?" she shouted. "Get the patients out!"

He hesitated, clutching the records close to his chest.

"I have to—I have to save these!"

Through the darkness, he saw her contempt, and was ashamed.

"I'll—I'll start on the Hudson Wing," he said.

They ran through the darkness, following the cries of fear from men and women whose worst nightmares had now been realised.

CHAPTER 35

Gregory felt his way through the darkness to try the door again, and found it open.

He hurried out into the corridor, where screams of terror echoed like inhuman spectres in a carnival house of horrors.

Which way?

Which way out?

He'd been sedated when they transferred him to the maximum-security ward and, without any light, Gregory was disoriented. He felt his way along the wall, following the sounds rising up from the floor below, before he remembered something important.

He was still a doctor, and owed a duty of care.

Though it went against every instinct of self-preservation, he doubled back and checked inside all the rooms he passed, to make sure nobody was left behind.

Finding them empty, he was about to head for the stairs when he tripped over something bulky which blocked his path.

He realised it was a person.

Fletcher had reached the upper landing, and had been in the process of checking the rooms when he'd collapsed. They would later learn that the cause was a congenital heart problem, the stress of the fire having brought on a massive and unexpected heart attack.

But Gregory didn't know that.

He only knew there was a man in need of help.

He checked for a pulse and found it weak, but that was good enough. The next problem was getting him downstairs. Fletcher was heavily-built and, although Gregory was a tall, athletic man himself, it would be a challenge to transport a dead weight three floors down to the exit. There was a service elevator, but it couldn't be used in a fire, especially now that the power had failed.

He was left with no choice.

Gregory dragged Fletcher towards the emergency stairs, then turned him, clasping both of the man's arms in a hard grip before taking a deep breath and lifting him up, so that he was leaning against his back. He kept a tight hold of the man's arms and pushed through the emergency door, feeling the night air blast his face as he began to make his slow, careful journey down the wrought-iron stairs with Fletcher on his back.

Outside, Kaufmann and some of the other staff had already congregated at the emergency point on the lawn with a majority of the patients. Spotting him, one of the other orderlies ran across to help and, when they did, the feeling of relief left Gregory light-headed.

They dragged Fletcher across the lawn to where the others were huddled—weeping and crying, shaking and muttering—and the nurses took over, administering first aid where they could.

Sweat was running down Gregory's face, blinding him, and he wiped it away with the edge of his tee-shirt, before looking at the others who cowered on the lawn.

"Where's Doctor Palmer?" he demanded. "Where's Lorena—and Megan?"

He could only see Kitty and Rosie amongst the crowd of men.

Doctor Kaufmann's eyes gleamed with terror.

"I can't go back inside," he muttered. "I—the fire—I can't go back—"

He was paralysed with fear, Gregory realised. He looked at the other nurses, who worked hard to keep Fletcher alive and the other patients safe, and made his decision.

"I'll go," he said, and took off at a sprint.

———

The fire raged in Overlook Wing, licking at the panelled walls, snaking its way over the paintings and wallpaper as it spread further towards the room where Naomi stood, engaged in a battle of wills.

"Megan, you have to come with me now—*please*."

The girl had completely shut down, fear and panic rendering her immobile, and severe depression telling her to let it happen.

"Megan, the fire's getting worse, we have to leave *now*!"

The girl continued to rock on her bed, and Naomi tried to grasp her arm, to pull her to safety. Suddenly, she lashed out, a glancing blow across the doctor's face which sent her stumbling to the floor.

Shaken, running out of time, Naomi dragged herself up to try again.

"Leave me alone!" Megan cried. "Just leave me here!"

She struggled against Naomi's arms, scratching and biting as the smoke grew heavier.

"Megan, you matter to me, and to all of us," Naomi said, trying not to succumb to panic. "Please, come with me now."

Through the darkness, above the sound of splitting wood and roaring fire, she heard the girl start to cry.

"Please," she wailed. "Just—just leave me here!"

The sound was heartbreaking, the source of it even more so, but Naomi needed the girl alive so they could tackle it another day.

After another brief battle, she took a firm hold of the girl's arms, pinning them behind her back.

"This is for your safety and mine," she said, and propelled her from the room.

Gregory made for the terrace doors at the back of the hospital.

They led into the eastern wing of the old house, beside the kitchen and dining area, avoiding the ballroom and the library on the south-eastern corner whose windows had already succumbed to the flames.

But, as he approached, he felt the heat like a wall, and knew the fire had spread too far for him to enter.

Quickly, he ran around the corner of the house, following the paved stone path until he reached the fire stairs on the north-east corner which he'd used to drag Fletcher to safety. He ran past them, further along the north wall to its western corner, where a second set of fire stairs awaited.

He grasped the rail, and took them two at a time.

Before he could reach the top, the door burst open and Naomi appeared with a struggling Megan by her side. She looked fit to collapse, the effort of strong-arming the girl combined with a lack of oxygen having taken their toll.

Spotting him, her eyes flared with hope, quickly extinguished.

"Michael, go back and stay with the others—"

He said nothing, and plucked Megan from her arms, throwing the girl over his shoulder with more speed than finesse.

"I'll take her," he managed, strapping an arm across the girl's legs so she couldn't kick out. "Where's Lorena?"

"I couldn't lift her," Naomi's voice wobbled. "I'll try again—"

"Come with me to safety," he said. "I'll go back for her."

She wanted to accept his help, and she desperately wanted to trust him, but his actions of the past few days couldn't be so easily forgotten.

"No, Michael. The fire service will be here soon—"

But there was no comforting siren approaching through the woods, and the nearest Fire Department was eight miles away, in Woodstock. On a good day, it would take at least ten minutes for them to arrive.

Long enough for a fire to destroy an entire mansion, if a person knew how to set it.

Gregory didn't stand around arguing, but hurried down the fire stairs and back across the lawn, where he deposited Megan beside the others.

"Michael, what about—"

Kaufmann started to call to him, but Gregory was already setting off again, covering the ground at speed.

When he returned to the fire stairs, he saw no sign of Naomi and knew instantly that she'd ignored his advice. He hurried upstairs again, feet clattering against the metalwork, and sucked in a deep breath before yanking open the door to the first level.

CHAPTER 36

Inside, it was a living hell.

The low-security ward of the Overlook Wing at Buchanan Hospital was engulfed in smoke, and getting worse. Flames had reached the far end of the corridor, ravaging the walls and spreading fast along the floor, crackling and snapping at the wood. Gregory took off his tee-shirt and tied it roughly around his face, before stepping into the wall of heat, eyes streaming as he moved through the darkness to find Lorena's room.

Then, he saw them.

Naomi dragged Lorena's inert body from an open doorway further along the corridor, coughing and spluttering as she inhaled black smoke.

Gregory moved fast, turning her away and pushing her towards the emergency stairs before reaching down to lift Lorena into his arms. His shoulder caught the edge of the burning wall as he passed, moving awkwardly with the unconscious woman in his arms, and he let out a sharp hiss of pain.

Every step was laboured as his lungs screamed for air, and his arms strained beneath the weight of the woman he held, but eventually they burst outside into the cool night air to find Naomi coughing and heaving, her face shiny with sweat and stained with smoke.

They struggled down the stairs, but they had only made it halfway before a figure appeared at the bottom.

"Doctor Gregory! Thank God—"

Agent Johnson rushed up the iron stairs, sending the metal shaking against its hinges.

"Here, let me help you—is she dead?"

Carefully, he transferred Lorena from Gregory's arms into his own.

"Still alive," Gregory rasped, feeling his whole body quivering with fatigue. "Her breathing is laboured, but she's still alive."

"Wait—" Naomi managed, drawing in several ragged breaths. "Who are you? Where are you taking her?"

"Special Agent Johnson, ma'am," he threw back over his shoulder. "Come on, let's get you all to safety."

FBI?

Naomi stared at his retreating back, then turned to Gregory. "I—"

"Let's go," he urged her. "Ask questions later, when there isn't a fire at my back."

They hurried after Agent Johnson, who carried Lorena with the competent arms of one who spent most weekends completing the Bureau's assault course for his own pleasure. Instead of joining the others on the lawn, he turned in the other direction and made for the road around the front of the hospital.

"We need to get you out of here as quickly as possible," he puffed. "There's a car waiting."

Naomi and Gregory limped after him.

"How did you know to be here?" Gregory asked, before he was overcome by another coughing fit.

"We heard about what happened with Tilda," Johnson said. "We've had a line on her for a while; her son has some bad gambling debts and we think Romano used that as leverage, the past couple of years. We got a tip that Romano was going to try and bust in to snatch Lorena himself, so we got up here as quickly as we could."

He continued to hurry across the elegant driveway, to where a dark SUV was parked and waiting for them.

"Wait—you can't just take her!" Naomi cried.

"She's coming into Witness Protection, ma'am," Johnson said. "If you could both accompany us for the time being, to look after her, we'll make sure you're returned safely."

Now that the smoke had cleared from his addled brain, Gregory put together the pieces of the jigsaw, and found they didn't quite fit.

"What happened to Hawk?" he asked, throwing out an arm to signal Naomi to stay back.

The man himself stepped out of the driver's seat and hurried around to open the back door as they approached, so Johnson could settle Lorena inside.

"*Hawk*?"

Gregory was incredulous.

"Why didn't you answer any of my calls? How did you know—"

He trailed off, as Johnson turned back to them, this time with a pistol trained at their heads.

"Get into the car," he said quietly. "Do it now, don't try to be a hero."

———

They passed the fire crew as they hurtled down the mountain road.

Lorena was still passed out, her body slumped against the side of the car, while the two FBI agents stared out of the windshield, barely acknowledging their presence.

"Where are you taking us?" Naomi asked.

The two agents looked at each other, then back at the road.

"You'll find out, soon enough," Hawk said.

Gregory caught his eye in the rearview mirror.

"Why did you do it?" he asked. "Why did you set the fire?"

When they remained silent, he gave a laugh that was pure bravado.

"Come on," he said. "What harm can it do, to tell me now?"

"That's what I always liked about you, Doc," Hawk said. "You get straight to the point and you don't try and kid yourself."

"I already know you don't believe in happy endings," Gregory said quietly, and thought of a little boy whose mother liked to carry watermelons.

Hawk grinned like a tiger.

"Maybe you're right," he said. "It won't do any harm, now."

He slowed the car to make a sharp left turn, which sent the three people on the back seat crashing to one side.

"Not everybody had a rich daddy, like you," Johnson said. "Some of us had to be resourceful."

Gregory said nothing, but tried to hold on to his stomach as the car pitched and swerved.

"When you finally get some money, you get a taste for it," Hawk said. "You spend it, you get some more…it gets to be an addiction."

"So you betrayed your badge and your country, to feed it?"

"Don't talk to me about *this country*," Johnson said, angrily. "My father gave his life in service to lady liberty, and where the hell did it leave him? Crippled, surviving on peanuts."

"You want to talk about corruption? Let me tell you something, Doc—working for the Bureau, it gets to be that you can't tell who're the good guys, and who're the bad guys, anymore."

Maybe you needed a refresher course, Gregory thought.

"When did you first meet Romano?" he asked.

"Five, maybe six years ago," Hawk said. "Bureau sent me in, undercover, to infiltrate the Romano Family and try to find a weak link we could try and flip. Instead, I offered Paolo a line back to the Bureau, in exchange for a modest fee for my partner and myself, which he gratefully accepted."

"Very enterprising," Gregory remarked.

"Thanks, Doc—I thought so, too. Anyway, I went back to Quantico and told them he'd made me, got myself assigned to BAU, in the Organised Crime division. Right at the centre of the action, you might say."

"So, what happened?" Gregory wondered aloud, and silently reached out a hand to hold Naomi's. She curled her fingers around his and held on tight.

"Just lately, Mr Romano has stopped sending his regular payments," Hawk said. "Now, as I've already told you, it is easy for a man to get used to a certain way of living, so I don't mind telling you that made us pretty angry. Didn't it?"

"It sure did," Johnson said, cheerfully. "After all we done for him, too."

Hawk tutted. "See, the thing is, when I first started getting to know the Romanos undercover, I did identify the weak link," he said, with a private smile. "Lorena and me, we got along like a house on fire—if you'll pardon the pun."

He laughed at his own joke.

"It didn't take much to strike up that friendship again, when the time came to remind Mr Romano why he should honour his commitments," Hawk continued. "He *needs* us, and he needs to remember that."

Gregory's mind boggled at the audacity of their plan, and he could hardly believe Paolo Romano would respond with anything other than violence.

"You wanted to prove that you could turn someone, for real," Gregory said, beginning to understand the extent of it. "You flipped Lorena and you planned to pick her up, but instead of taking her into Witness Protection, you'd let Romano know about it and kill her, instead—after you'd made your point. Is that it?"

"Not far off," Hawk said. "Only, the stupid bitch disappeared."

Gregory realised they had no idea why Lorena had been at Buchanan Hospital, and stole a glance at Naomi. Looking at the two women, he wondered if he was imagining the family resemblance, or if there wasn't a certain curve to the cheek and jaw that gave them away.

"Don't you think Romano will be angry?"

"Paolo is a businessman," Hawk said. "He understands our reasons, and respects them. We had a nice, cordial chat with Mr Romano, and he understands why we felt there was no other option but to remind him of our agreement."

Johnson turned around with another of his unnerving smiles.

"Actually, you really did us a favour, interrupting Tilda like that. Don't know what we'd have done, if she got to Lorena first."

"Yeah, pretty decent of you, Doc," Hawk intoned. "Paolo tried to sort out the problem on his own, but now he knows everybody needs a friendly, neighbourhood Fed, when the chips are down."

The two men laughed.

They were driving along a rough-surfaced road now, which led through the Overlook Wild Forest, and Gregory wondered how many times desperate men and women had committed dark deeds in the shadows of the trees, never to be discovered.

Naomi was breathing hard now, trying to control her panic, and Lorena was beginning to stir on her other side. As they took another turn down an unmarked road, deep into the depths of the forest, he wondered if it would have been better if she had remained unconscious throughout.

CHAPTER 37

"Hey, Rena! Thought you'd never wake up in time," Hawk said.

Lorena found she could barely speak; her throat and chest having been dealt a double blow over the past forty-eight hours. She looked around the car in confusion, wondering why Naomi and Michael were sitting with her contact from the FBI.

"What's happening, Mason? What's going on?"

It was the first time Gregory had heard Agent Hawk's first name, and somehow the mundane quality of it didn't suit the man.

"I'm taking you back to your husband, where you belong," he said.

"What?" she croaked. "But, then, he'll know—"

"He already knows, sweetheart," Johnson said. "Did you think you'd found a way out? Is that it?"

Both men laughed.

"Maybe you can clear something up for us, Rena. 'Michael' here thinks you were faking those demons to get yourself admitted to the Buchanan," Hawk said. "Is he right?"

Lorena looked at the woman seated beside her, and thought again that she'd been to blame for putting her child at risk. The least she could do now was allow Naomi to remain ignorant of the kind of family she came from. She could go on telling herself nice stories about the woman who'd birthed her, which wouldn't be sullied by anything as grubby as the truth.

Gregory watched the emotional turmoil passing over Lorena's face and wondered what she would decide.

"The demon I saw was real," Lorena said, and turned to look out of the window to hide her tears.

"Turns out you not always right after all," Hawk said, eyeing Gregory in the mirror.

"I never claimed to be," Gregory replied.

In the reflection of the window, Lorena sent him a grateful smile.

They lapsed into silence, until presently they came to a clearing where a car was already parked and waiting for them.

"Looks like we're late," Hawk said, bringing the car to a halt.

He twisted around in his seat to face the three of them.

"I want you to know, this isn't personal," he said. "What is it they say in the Family, Rena? *It's just business*."

"You're not in the Family," she whispered. "You don't understand how things work at all."

"Looks like I understand them much better than you. Look," he said, pointing through the windshield. "Your loving husband's come to meet you."

Lorena closed her eyes, and prepared herself for what was to come.

"As for the two of you," Hawk said, "I didn't plan things this way. I just needed to know for sure whether Lorena was sick. You know your problem, Doc? You just don't know when to let it go."

"Seems a shame to lose you, princess," Johnson said to Naomi. "I never like waste, but them's the rules. You've seen us now, and we can't have that, can we?"

"What happened to Bill?" Gregory asked, though he feared he knew the answer already.

"He had a little accident with the front of my car," Hawk said. "Can't believe he's still going, but I guess you Brits know how to hang around."

So he was alive, at least for now, Gregory thought. If things turned out badly for them, at least he would know his friend was still alive, somewhere out there.

Across the clearing, the other car flashed his headlights.

"Time to go," Hawk said.

Hawk and Johnson stepped out of the car and held open the back doors.

"Get out," Johnson ordered.

The shot came from nowhere, and caught him in the centre of his skull.

Blood spattered over the roof of the car, pattering like rain, and Gregory watched the man's eyes die long before his body hit the ground.

Hawk had barely turned before a second shot was fired, catching him in the chest and then another in the throat to finish the job, in case he was wearing a protective vest. Night birds flew up into the sky, squawking loudly, their wings flapping in protest.

Naomi screamed, and Lorena threw herself over her daughter, forming a human shield. Gregory ducked his head behind the front seat and saw in his peripheral vision that Johnson's firearm had landed close by. If he made a grab for it, he might just reach it.

There was no time to act, before the doors of the other car opened and four men stepped out, as well as a fifth gunman who'd positioned himself across the clearing.

"Go get your mother," Arturo said to his grandson. "You've kept your side of the bargain."

Luca kissed both of his grandfather's cheeks and hurried across the clearing to retrieve his mother from the car.

When she saw her son approaching, Lorena began to cry.

"Luca? Why are you here?"

"It's time for a new life, Mamma," he said. Then, turning to the other two, he made a brief calculation. The deal hadn't included any witnesses.

"I'll speak on your behalf," he told them. But he made no promises.

They watched as Luca took his mother's arm and led her across the clearing to where her father waited with three of his men.

"Papa? What are you doing here? Where is Paolo?"

Arturo hardened his heart.

"Lorena, you betrayed your family—you have betrayed all the families," he said, and let his words hang on the air. "But I betrayed you first. I know that, now, Rena."

Like a prisoner in the dock, Lorena closed her eyes and awaited his judgment.

"Luca's brokered a deal on your behalf," he said, and her eyes flew open again. "It's somethin' all the families have approved, and after this day you must leave and never return."

She nodded. "What's the deal?"

Arturo led her around to the trunk of the car and instructed one of his men to open it.

It popped open to reveal Paolo Romano, bound and gagged, smelling strongly of faeces after soiling himself several times during the trip from New Jersey.

"This man's father broke the peace between the families—he was a warmonger and his son was the profiteer," Arturo said, and spat onto the ground. "I sold you into marriage, Lorena, for the sake of peace between our families. Instead, this man drove you to madness."

Lorena didn't bother to argue the point.

"Once he's gone, every family will take a share of New Jersey territory."

"And Luca?" she asked, looking over at her young son. "What will happen to him?"

"Luca goes with you," Arturo said. "You will never speak of the family again. Understand?"

She nodded her agreement.

"This will send a message to any other ambitious men," Arturo said, proudly. "It may be three or thirty years, but the son will pay for the sins of his father."

He held out a hand to his bodyguard, who placed an automatic handgun into the palm.

Arturo set the weapon, taking his time to enjoy Paolo's frantic, muffled howls but, then, at the last moment, turned to his daughter.

"This honour should be yours," he said.

Lorena stared into the eyes of the man who'd abused her for more than thirty years; who'd killed and maimed, cheated and lied. He was an animal in her eyes; one of those fighting dogs that couldn't live amongst normal dogs anymore without lashing out.

Eventually, they were put to sleep.

Lupara bianca, she whispered, as she closed the trunk.

CHAPTER 38

"What's happening?" Naomi took Gregory's hand again, and gripped it hard.

"I think Luca's bargaining for our lives."

They stared out of the window and, for a minute, they might have been at a drive-in movie, or sitting on a sofa somewhere watching a TV show about the Mob.

"I'm sorry," Naomi said softly.

"What for?"

"I'm sorry I didn't believe you, when you tried to tell me the truth."

"Don't be," he said. "As far as the FBI story goes, if I were in your shoes, I don't know that I would have believed me either."

She let out a slightly hysterical laugh. "In my defence, you did sound completely insane."

"Hardly any different to normal," he smiled.

Then, he grew serious. If the situation was about to go badly south, there were things he needed to say.

"I want to thank you," he said. "You helped me to understand myself better, and to understand how to forgive. That's an incredible gift, and I'm grateful."

Naomi turned to face him, and smiled at his unkempt appearance. Gregory's dark hair was ruffled, and his face smudged with smoke. His white T-shirt would certainly never be white again, and she noticed, for the first time, an angry red gash on his upper right arm.

"What happened there?" she asked.

"Caught it on a wall."

She thought of how selfless he had been throughout the ordeal, and before it, when he'd been entirely alone.

"I suppose I should start calling you Doctor Gregory, now, shouldn't I?"

His lips curved.

"Alexander, or Michael," he said. "They're one and the same."

"But neither of them is my patient any longer."

There was a crackling silence.

"No, neither of them is."

He searched her face, then gently cradled it in his hands before lowering his head to brush his lips over hers. Just the merest of kisses, but enough to be a sweet memory, or a sweet beginning, depending on how the hammer fell.

When it was over, they saw that the Lucchese had come to their decision. Luca and his mother made their way across the clearing, and stepped back into the car.

Luca started the engine and performed a fast U-turn, sending small streams of dust into the night air.

"Don't look behind," Lorena said. "Only forwards."

———

Luca drove for an hour without stopping, until they came to the city of Poughkeepsie, in the southern quarter of the Hudson Valley. There, he pulled into a service station on the outskirts of town and drove around the back, to where several other cars were parked.

"This is our stop, Ma," he said, and then turned to the other two. "You won't have any more trouble from the Families."

"Are you sure?" Gregory felt it was a pertinent question to ask.

Luca shrugged. "I had to tell them I was going to waste you myself," he said. "So, keep your mouth shut and lie low for a while. They don't know your names and didn't get a good look. They're happy enough."

Gregory didn't feel entirely satisfied with that assurance, but it was the best they were going to get. "Where will you go now?" he asked them.

Luca nodded towards a blue station wagon, inside which a young man by the name of Felix was waiting for them.

He turned to his mother with a worried expression.

"Ma, I never told you—" he began.

"You think I don't know my boy? I've always known," Lorena said, raising a hand to cup his cheek. "Just tell me, is he good to you?"

Luca nodded.

"And does he like cannoli?"

Her son grinned.

"Then we'll get along just fine. You head on over and I'll join you in just a minute."

Once he'd left, Lorena spoke to Gregory and Naomi.

"I want to thank you both, and to apologise for the danger I put you in," she said.

"Will you be all right?" Naomi asked.

Lorena looked into the woman's deep brown eyes that were so like her own, and wanted so much to embrace the daughter she'd lost. But this woman was somebody else's daughter now; somebody who had obviously done a wonderful job of making her the person she was—perhaps a better job than she could have done. Naomi Palmer had known a legitimate life, free from harm, and filled with love and opportunity. Lorena could not, hand on heart, say that she would have been able to guarantee all of those things.

Except her love.

Naomi would always have that.

Lorena reached across to cup her cheek, as she had done with her son moments before.

"Your mama would be proud," she said, and then snatched her hand away before she could change her mind.

"You're a good boy," she said, offering her hand to Gregory. "Your mama would have been proud too, if she had the sense. Take it from this one instead, okay?"

She reached for the door, then remembered one final thing.

"I left the recipe for the cannoli in the kitchen drawer," she said. "Third from the left, by the oven. Those people, my friends at the hospital, they've been like family to me. They deserve to know the recipe, so I hope it survived the fire."

After that, she left and didn't look back.

CHAPTER 39

Two Weeks Later

"Are we nearly there?" Douglas asked. "My arse is starting to fall asleep."

Gregory smiled and continued to steer the hire car along the winding mountain road towards the gates of Buchanan Hospital.

It was a blistering hot day, and the sun beamed long, dappled rays of light through the trees, which flickered against the windscreen.

"How does it feel, coming back here?" Douglas asked.

It had been a difficult couple of weeks for both of them, each recovering in their own ways from what would go down in history as their most eventful trip to Quantico yet.

"It feels... oddly, like coming home. I might have been an impostor, but the people at the hospital made me feel welcome. I'll never forget it, or them."

Douglas had noticed a significant change in his friend, ever since Gregory had turned up at his bedside at Georgetown University Hospital. Never had there been a more welcome sight, he recalled, than seeing his friend standing there wielding a helium balloon that said, 'Get Well Soon.'

Presently, the hospital materialised up ahead. It was not quite its former self, having suffered severe fire damage to the interior and some minor structural damage, particularly in its northern wing, but there was no mistaking the clock tower and gable ends, nor the view, which was incomparable.

"Hang on a minute," Douglas said. "If I'd known this is where you'd been staying, I wouldn't have felt half as guilty about getting myself run over."

Gregory snorted. "Next time, you can be the one who goes undercover. I'd like to see you trying to convince a team of psychiatrists that you are really an FBI agent."

Douglas chuckled. "It can't have been all bad," he said.

As they approached the entrance to the hospital, Gregory caught sight of Naomi, stepping outside the front door to greet them.

"No," he said. "It certainly wasn't all bad."

Naomi had brought a folding wheelchair for Douglas, who she happened to know was still recovering from a broken leg and some cracked ribs, amongst other minor ailments.

Gregory walked around the car to help his friend, and smiled at her on the way.

"It's good to see you again," he said. "I don't know if you've met my friend, Professor Bill Douglas?"

She gave Gregory a withering look, knowing fine well he was laughing at her previous disbelief in his wild story about knowing the man.

"It's a pleasure to meet you, Professor Douglas," she said. "We're so glad you could visit."

They made their way around to the lawn, where tables had been set out for a summer garden party, loaded with food of all kinds—including cannoli baked to Lorena's special recipe. A construction team had been working around the clock for the past two weeks to repair the worst of the fire damage, while the patients were moved into the Hudson wing, which was in much better shape. Fine weather had allowed them to spend more time outside, where Naomi had organised all manner of alternative therapy classes including music, art, and movement.

"Where's Kaufmann?" Gregory asked, noting that the hospital administrator was absent from the party.

"He tendered his resignation a couple of days after the fire," she said. "I think the Board were planning to fire him, anyway."

"Does that mean there's a vacancy available? You would be wonderful," he said, sincerely.

"They've offered me the position," she said. "I've agreed to take it in the interim, but I don't know whether I'll stay here in the long term."

"Congratulations," Gregory said, swallowing his own disappointment.

What did he think would happen? That she'd uproot her life and come to live in the UK?

He was dreaming, again.

"Have you heard anything more about Lorena Romano?" Douglas asked.

Naomi shook her head.

"Nothing," she said. "There's been nothing about it in the news, either."

She thought of Luca's advice to them before he left, and decided that was probably a good thing.

"Well, hello, Alexander!"

Kitty Steenberg was dressed to impress, in a long, floating gown made entirely of leopard print chiffon. So as not to *over*dress for the occasion, she'd limited herself to only one hat.

"Hello, Mrs Steenberg," Gregory said, still finding it hard to believe this woman had been a killer. "How are you feeling today?"

"Oh, perfectly well, dear. I'm *so* pleased to see you, and—oh, look! Here's my Terrence, now! I told you, he'd be along to collect me."

She beamed at Douglas, who, being restricted to a wheelchair, was unable to run away.

Gregory grinned, and wandered over to where Harry and Marco were seated, tucking into bowls of ice cream and jelly with gusto.

"Well, would you look what the cat's dragged in," Harry said, dribbling ice cream down his beard. "What happened, kid? We thought you'd bought it in the fire."

Gregory smiled. "I'm going home soon," he said. "But first, I wanted to stop by and visit my old friends."

For once, Harry didn't try to misunderstand.

"Won't be the same without you around here," he said gruffly. "Means I gotta speak to Marco, for one thing."

"Oh yeah?" Marco said. "Well, how d'ya think I feel about—"

"Actually, I brought you both a little something," Gregory said, interrupting one of their spats. "Call it a going-away present."

He reached inside a brown paper bag and pulled out two baseball caps, each bearing the logo of their favourite team.

"Here," Gregory said. "It'll stop you getting burned on your bald patch, Harry."

"These Brits," Harry said. "They think they're so superior, with their full heads of hair."

"Never did like them, myself," Marco agreed.

Both men grinned and settled the caps on their heads.

They stayed awhile, until the sun fell low in the sky and Gregory knew the time had come when he must say goodbye. He visited each of the tables, wishing a fond farewell to all the residents, and then turned to the woman who waited patiently beneath the shade of the oak tree.

Naomi smiled as he crossed the lawn, and thought how different he seemed, and yet so much the same. There was a confidence that hadn't been there before, but the kindness and the compassion were unchanged.

"Time to go?" she asked.

He nodded. "We've got a flight from JFK tonight."

"Come back and visit us, some time," she said.

"Why don't you come to London, instead?" he offered. "I'd like to take you dancing."

Naomi smiled slowly.

"I've never been to London," she said. "Perhaps it's time I did."

Gregory watched the fall of sunlight on her hair, and thought back to their time in the ballroom. He needed no hallucinogen to imagine stars around this woman, he thought. Naomi Palmer carried her own light around her.

He reached for her hand and raised it to his lips.

"Goodbye," he said.

Across the lawn, Harry and Marco wandered over to where Douglas was sipping the last of his pineapple punch.

"So? What're you in for, Champ?" Harry asked him.

Douglas smiled politely.

"Oh, I'm just here visiting, with my friend."

Harry and Marco looked at one another, then back at him.

"Yeah, us too," they said, erupting into raucous laughter.

"I thought you were here for the fresh air," Harry said to his friend.

"Nah, you gotta be kiddin'," Marco said. "I'm here for the bird-watching."

They laughed again, and Harry's signature hoot was so loud, Douglas feared it would bring on an avalanche.

"Nice caps," he said, once they'd recovered themselves.

The two men patted their heads.

"Thanks," Harry replied. "They were a present from a friend of ours—Michael. You know him?"

"More and more, every day," Douglas said, with a smile.

EPILOGUE

The following Monday morning, Gregory returned to Southmoor Hospital.

It was a desolate place for some, he supposed, but it reminded him of a kind of 'Forbidden Kingdom', surrounded by a high wall through which only a few were allowed to enter. The reality might have been less glamorous than those golden turrets in Beijing, but Southmoor was nonetheless a kind of walled city that inspired a similar degree of awe. It had been built along organised, Victorian lines, with a number of wings sprouting off the central blocks, where each of its alarmed doors opened outwards, and all of its windows were barred—though they lacked the intricate ironwork enjoyed by the residents of Buchanan Hospital. On an ordinary day, Gregory might have been settling back into the comfortable routine of patients and clinical care meetings but, instead, he made his way to the Clinical Director's office.

Doctor Parminder Aggarwal was a thin woman with a big smile and an enthusiasm for her work that far outweighed any remuneration she might have received at the end of every month. Her cheerful demeanour and no-nonsense capability were qualities in high demand at a place like Southmoor, whilst her compassion for the men and women in her charge never failed to be an inspiration.

It was therefore with some considerable regret that Gregory stood on the threshold of her office, staring for a moment at the small brass plaque that bore her name.

He knocked, and entered when she called out a friendly "Come in!"

Inside, she smiled at him and walked around the desk to bestow a friendly peck on each cheek.

"Have a seat, Alex," she said. "How was your holiday?"

How long have you got?

"Oh, you know," he said. "Eye-opening."

"I've heard the scenery on the East Coast is beautiful," she sighed. "Now, then. What was it you wanted to speak to me about?"

Gregory looked down at the small sheaf of papers he held in his hand, and laid them on the table in front of her, like an offering.

"I've put it all in writing, so you have my statement on record," he said quietly.

Parminder frowned down at the papers.

"What's this all about, Alex?"

"Professional misconduct," he said simply. "And my apology for it."

She listened while he set out the truth of his relationship with Cathy Jones, his mother, and what had led him to make such a poor error of judgment in choosing to accept her as his patient. He made no excuses, and spoke only sparingly of the details of his childhood.

After he'd finished, Parminder pressed her hands together.

"Thank you for being so honest with me, Alex," she said. "The first thing I need to say is that I have a duty to report this to the Hospital Board, who may refer it to the regulator."

It was only what he had expected.

"I understand," he said.

"The second thing I need to say is that I'll be putting in a recommendation that you take three months' sabbatical leave, pending any inquiry. I presume you kept records?"

He nodded, wondering why she hadn't recommended that he be suspended.

Parminder leaned forward and spoke gently to him.

"Finally, let me ask you this, Alex—why do you think I wanted to work in the field of psychology?"

It was a rhetorical question, but he answered anyway.

"To help people."

"Exactly right. I know it was the same for you, too. Do you think that desire to help people ends when my last patient leaves the treatment room, or I clock out of this place and go home for fishfingers and chips with my kids?"

She shook her head.

"I know you've been troubled, Alex. It's been a concern to me for a while, and—do you know?—I was starting to wonder whether you'd tell me something much worse than a story about an abused little boy who took the chance, one day, to find out some answers. You broke the rules, Alex, but you're not a bad man. Please don't forget that, because I won't."

Gregory cleared his throat.

"Thank you, Parminder."

"I can't make you any promises, Alex, except one—whatever the Board decides, you'll always have friends here at Southmoor."

He found Douglas waiting for him at the pizzeria, down on the high street.

"Here?" Gregory asked, looking around at the red-and-white-checked tablecloths and artificial olive branches hanging from beams in the ceiling.

Dean Martin crooned from a set of ancient speakers tucked behind a wine casket.

"I thought, given our recent experience, we'd celebrate being several thousand miles away from our Italian-American friends, by eating an Italian-American meal."

"Why not," Gregory said, pulling back a chair.

"So? How did it go?"

"As expected," Gregory replied. "Parminder was very understanding, and is recommending I take a three-month sabbatical."

"Perfect," Douglas said quietly, from behind his menu.

"What for?"

"Other projects," Douglas said, wriggling his preposterous eyebrows.

"Not a chance."

"I haven't told you what it is, yet."

"You don't need to," Gregory replied. "The answer's still no."

Douglas began whistling an old Frank Sinatra tune, and wondered when the most opportune moment would be to tell his friend he'd decided to reopen the Profiling Unit.

Maybe after they'd had some cannoli.

ALEX GREGORY WILL RETURN IN SUMMER 2020…

If you would like to be kept up to date with new releases from LJ Ross, please complete an e-mail contact form on her Facebook page or website, **www.ljrossauthor.com**

AUTHOR'S NOTE

The idea for *Bedlam* first came about many years ago, when I was eighteen and living my first semester of university in London at King's College Halls—a residential building for students located in the south-east of the city, not far from the Maudsley Hospital. Those halls were a cool, forty-five-minute bus journey to the nearest lecture hall, which made for a miserable journey at seven-thirty on a Monday morning, following 'Sunday Night Shots' the day before.

But I digress.

The Maudsley was, and still is, one of the most respected psychiatric hospitals in the world, and the largest mental health training facility in the United Kingdom. It so happens that the bus stop I used to make my daily excursion into the centre of town was located directly opposite its main entrance.

Soon after my parents left me in KCH, as it had come affectionately to be known, I made my way along with the rest of my peers to catch a double-decker bus along the Camberwell Road. There followed my first encounter with 'Mary'.

Mary liked to carry lots of empty shopping bags. She never told me why, or how many, or what they meant to her, but she did enjoy whacking me with them, whenever she happened to see me at the bus stop. There followed an elaborate game of cat and mouse, where I would go to increasingly careful lengths to avoid the lady with the bags, having decided my face must resemble that of her greatest enemy. I remember one particular coup on Mary's part, in which she had already boarded the bus at the previous stop, and therefore was waiting on-board to whack me with said plastic bags, rather than keeping to anything so predictable as our usual meeting place.

At first, I found this behaviour alarming, then hurtful, I suppose—but then my mother (a psychologist) suggested that the lady may not be trying to hurt me, but to get my attention for some reason. All along, I'd been looking at things from a certain vantage point, whereas, at least from her perspective, there may have been a much more benevolent reason for the bag-whacking.

I decided to test this theory the very next day.

Only, I never saw Mary again.

It's very strange that, of all the experiences in my life, that episode with 'Mary' should have stayed in my mind—but it has. Long afterwards, I wondered how she was faring, and regretted never stopping to engage her in more fruitful conversation. We are all people, despite our differences, and we view the world through the prism of our own understanding. This early understanding formed the foundation when I turned my mind to writing *Bedlam*, in which I hoped to highlight the similarities between all of us, rather than the differences.

I remember my university days with fondness, as I do the years that followed them, but I was always fascinated by the field of psychology—so much so, I completed a Postgraduate Diploma in Psychology whilst I was writing my first book, *Holy Island*, and was expecting my son, Ethan (I am of the school of thought whereby distraction is the key to a happy pregnancy, although I'm reliably informed that chocolate works equally as well as a diploma in psychology). It's a broad field, and all I have is a broad understanding, but as a writer of human traits and an observer of people in general, I hoped in *Bedlam* to craft a tale of one man's road to redemption. I hoped that my hero, Doctor Gregory, would learn he was not alone; that he was loved, and able to live a full life.

The setting for *Bedlam* takes its inspiration not only from the hospital of the same name in the UK, but from several mansion houses in the Catskill Mountains—which are beautiful, if you should ever have the chance to visit. The exterior of the fictional Buchanan Hospital was inspired by the Overlook Mountain House Ruins (not to be confused with Stephen King's 'Overlook Hotel'!), which is little more than the beautiful skeleton of a house near the summit of Overlook Mountain, which rises over three thousand feet above the town of Woodstock. Further inspiration for the interior and exterior of Buchanan Hospital was taken from Skene Manor, and if you would like to have a visual representation of the kind of place I had in mind, that would be a good starting point.

Quantico is, of course, a place very much represented in popular culture, and so I was keen not to spend too much time at the Training Academy, but rather more time in the village itself. I have always been partial to writing 'small town' settings, and this was no exception.

As for the Mafia scenes…well, they were a lot of fun to write. I often spoke the dialogue aloud, and my husband tells me I sound a lot like 'Mickey Blue Eyes'.

I hope you enjoyed the story, and your travels around the Catskills…

Until next time.

LJ ROSS
May 2020

ABOUT THE AUTHOR

LJ Ross is an international bestselling author, best known for creating atmospheric mystery and thriller novels, including the DCI Ryan series of Northumbrian murder mysteries which have sold over five million copies worldwide.

Her debut, *Holy Island*, was released in January 2015 and reached number one in the UK and Australian charts. Since then, she has released a further eighteen novels, fifteen of which have been top three global bestsellers and twelve of which have been UK #1 bestsellers. Louise has garnered an army of loyal readers through her storytelling and, thanks to them, several of her books reached the coveted #1 spot whilst only available to pre-order ahead of release.

Louise was born in Northumberland, England. She studied undergraduate and postgraduate Law at King's College, University of London and then abroad in Paris and Florence. She spent much of her working life in London, where she was a lawyer for a number of years until taking the decision to change career and pursue her dream to write. Now, she writes full time and lives with her husband and son in Northumberland. She enjoys reading all manner of books, travelling and spending time with family and friends.

If you enjoyed reading *Bedlam*, please consider leaving a review online.

If you enjoyed *Bedlam*, why not try the best-selling DCI Ryan Mysteries by LJ Ross?

HOLY ISLAND

A DCI RYAN MYSTERY (Book #1)

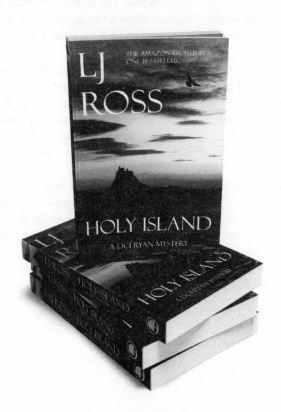

Detective Chief Inspector Ryan retreats to Holy Island seeking sanctuary when he is forced to take sabbatical leave from his duties as a homicide detective. A few days before Christmas, his peace is shattered, and he is thrust back into the murky world of murder when a young woman is found dead amongst the ancient ruins of the nearby Priory.

When former local girl Dr Anna Taylor arrives back on the island as a police consultant, old memories swim to the surface making her confront her difficult past. She and Ryan struggle to work together to hunt a killer who hides in plain sight, while pagan ritual and small-town politics muddy the waters of their investigation.

Murder and mystery are peppered with a sprinkling of romance and humour in this fast-paced crime whodunnit set on the spectacular Northumbrian island of Lindisfarne, cut off from the English mainland by a tidal causeway.

LOVE READING?

JOIN THE CLUB...

Join the LJ Ross Book Club to connect with a thriving community of fellow book lovers! To receive a free monthly newsletter with exclusive author interviews and giveaways, sign up at www.ljrossauthor.com or follow the LJ Ross Book Club on social media:

🐦 #LJBookClubTweet

f @LJRossAuthor

📷 @ljrossauthor